HOW TO GET A
Girlfriend

Paper Road Press
www.paperroadpress.co.nz

Published by Paper Road Press 2022

A catalogue record for this book is available from the National Library of New Zealand Te Puna Mātauranga o Aotearoa.

ebook ISBN 978-1-99-115038-7 paperback 978-1-99-115032-5
hardcover 978-1-99-115039-4

HOW TO GET A
Girlfriend

WHEN YOU'RE A
TERRIFYING
MONSTER

**PAPER
ROAD
PRESS**

In the constantly changing void of the Endless Dimension, there is no such thing as *people*. There is only one person – or perhaps 'being' would be a better word. The constant, hungering entity that both is and fills the entire dimension: the Endless itself. Fragments of the Endless sometimes fracture off, spattering free like bubbles in a galactic pot of porridge, but they are quickly absorbed again, and anything they learnt or thought or felt while they were separated is gobbled back up into the hungering one-ness.

Except for one.

She didn't remember how it had happened. One moment, she hadn't been anything at all; the next, she was. She had *edges*. Something between the Endless and this new, separate thing that was *her*. And with those edges and this new her-ness, a sudden and desperate desire not to be sucked back into eternal, omniscient obscurity.

The Endless wanted her back, no question about that. But she (she! An individual!) was still very small, and as long as she didn't *do* anything particularly noticeable, it was apparently difficult for the Endless to notice her.

The first time an interdimensional portal opened into the Endless, she thought it would provide good cover. The portal was very noticeable; next to it, she was even more likely to be overlooked. Even when the Endless manifested enormous eyeballs to peer at the portal, its gaze slid over her as though she didn't exist.

Excellent.

She didn't pay much attention to the portal the first few times it popped in and out of existence after that. It was enough that it attracted attention away from her, as she experimented with her edges and what she could do with the body – *her* body – inside them.

The Endless was full of shapes. It made and remade itself constantly, and fragments of it were forever sloughing off, devouring one another, and being reabsorbed by the whole again. She remembered a lot of the shapes from when she'd been part of the Endless, but none of them were right, and not just because it turned out to be very difficult to make your own shape when there was only *you* to make it.

None of the shapes she remembered were *her*. She didn't even really know what she was going to be, yet, but she was fiercely, confusedly jealous of it. And each experimental skin and limb and sensory apparatus brought her closer to herself.

One day, just as she had succeeded in creating a tentacle and was waving it around, the portal flared. The rippling surface between the five points that outlined its shape against the Endless changed colour as a shadow formed at its centre. The shadow darkened, grew larger, and something pushed through from the other side.

Not something. Her edges sparked. A ... a *someone*.

A someone with a flattish, paleish face, one blunt nose, two lidded eyes and a crest of dark hair. The bottom half of her face split, but not like aspects of the Endless split, forming and reforming along seams that changed position from moment to moment. This was an existing hole in the face, stretching wide as she stepped through the portal. Stepped through on legs. A body! A living body that moved through the world without changing its form!

She was suddenly, horribly self-conscious. She manifested another eyeball on the end of her tentacle and used it to look down at herself. Her body was ... not like the newcomer's. It had too many limbs, to start with. Small skittery limbs. She'd made a lot for practice, but now they were too many.

And her body had too many eyes, too, if the two the newcomer had were the number people were meant to have.

And a tentacle.

The newcomer didn't have *any* tentacles.

She skittered down until only her tentacle-eye was visible over the solid surface in front of the portal. From there, she watched as the strange new being twisted its head this way and that, its mouth still stretched wide and its eyes darting around as though it were searching for something.

"Fantastic," the creature breathed, and stepped back through the portal.

Her heart thudded. She suddenly had a heart to thud. It seemed to fill her entire body.

All at once, she knew two things.

First, she needed to make herself a new body. Something more like the urgently, wonderfully active creature she had just seen.

Second … she *had* to see that creature again.

Despite being separated from the Endless, the fragment still had its memories. At least, as many of them as could fit in her far smaller mind. She rifled through them as the portal dimmed. Before long, she found what she was looking for.

The portal-creature was what was known as a *human*.

The Endless had lots of memories of humans. Most of them were consumed memories from when a part of the Endless had split off, large enough to have its own goals and be able to carry them out. Usually, when a piece of the Endless got that big, its goals involved breaking through to another dimension and turning the inhabitants into mindless thralls. And the dimension where these *humans* lived was a particular favourite.

This did make it difficult for her to figure out what humans were like, given most of the memories involved screaming.

Still, there was enough to give her a good idea of what to do next.

If becoming an individual was the most exciting thing the fragment

4

had ever done, the *human* was the most exciting thing she'd ever seen. And if she wanted it to stick around for longer next time … she probably shouldn't look like the sort of beings that had spent the last couple of millennia trying to terrorise its dimension.

She wasn't sure how much time passed as she concentrated. The bodies she had made for herself previously were soft inside and out, occasional experiments into scales and antennae notwithstanding. To be anything like a *human* was a whole new challenge. Two jointed arms, with five bony tentacles on the end of each. Two legs, also jointed. She tried over and over, but couldn't figure out how to balance on them. They kept collapsing. And then there was the sort of oblongish shape in the middle. One head, two eyes…

She was in the middle of trying to figure out how the limbs connected to the oblongish middle bit when the portal began to glow again.

She had a mouth by this point, so she was able to make a strangled "Aaargh" noise as she tried to pull the rest of her new body together. Arms, she told herself. Arms and … legs … and … how did human noses work? How many eyes again? Should she make some spares, just in case?

The portal blooped, and the human popped through again.

Her heart fluttered. The human was so … *solid*. Now that she could get a better look at the visitor, she could tell – based on her borrowed memories – that the human was a she, as well.

An *incredible* she.

The human's limbs knew exactly where they were meant to be and how their jointed-ness worked. Her eyes were incredibly non-bulbous, and not even slightly on tentacles. And they were hardly bloodshot at all! Even their colour was exotically unchanging. She felt as though she could stare into them for hours and not get even a glimpse of uncanny light flaring from their depths, or a bubbling, glittering madness hinting at mysteries beyond all mortal ken.

Which was perfect.

Because, as her heart was telling her, if anyone was going to make this human's eyes glimmer with unearthly madness, it was going to be her.

Feathery cilia spread from her skin. Without any input from her, they vibrated against one another, making a soft trilling noise.

She froze. She had never made a *noise* before.

"Woo! Houston, we have landfall!" The human looked down to where her feet were resting on a coil of the Endless. It gooped slightly beneath her. "Well. Something-fall, anyway. Wow!"

The human picked up her feet one by one and the lonely fragment looked on, fascinated, as her body readjusted itself to allow for the movement without altering its shape.

The human had a skeleton underneath, didn't she?

She thought about adjusting her eyes to see through the human's surrounding flesh to the bones beneath, to see how they worked, but that seemed rude. They hardly knew each other. She didn't know much about human customs, but skeletons had to be private, or else why would they be so carefully wrapped up?

If she were more powerful, and the human agreed, she could arrange the human's atoms for her, make her flesh invisible or insubstantial as fog…

If she were more powerful. She felt the tug of the Endless plucking at her edges.

Anyway, even if she *were* more powerful, that seemed like more of a – she hunted through the impressions she'd gathered of human customs, outside the screaming – more of a 'third date' sort of thing.

"Gidday!" the human said, stretching her mouth over her teeth. The fragment waited for the smile to stretch all the way around the human's skull, revealing teeth where no teeth should be, and felt a thrill when she realised it wasn't going to happen. The human was completely, incredibly unchanging.

And looking at her.

She gulped. Her new limbs wanted to curl inwards and drag her away somewhere to hide.

But…

She wanted the human to stick around. Step one of that was *look like something worth sticking around for*, which – well, the human hadn't run screaming at the sight of her, which was a start. Step two was … was…

Conversation.

The mouth she'd created went dry. Was it meant to do that?

She tried to say 'Hello', but all that came out was a low hiss.

7

"I'm Sian. Are you the welcoming committee?" the human asked chirpily.

Sian. A name like the sound of skin brushing against skin. Soft and intimate.

She needed a name as well, didn't she? Humans had names. *People* had names.

What about the noise her cilia had made? Trill. Trillin. Trillin sound almost like a name, didn't it?

Sian was still grinning as her eyes travelled down the body Trillin had manifested. "Nice tentacles."

Trillin looked down at herself. Her heart sank. She knew she had trouble with legs, but in all her experimenting she'd never gotten it this wrong before.

Sian's skin was still tingling from stepping through the portal. All the hair on her body and possibly the hair on her head, who knew, was standing on end. She imagined each hair trying to weave itself into her spellsuit, like it wanted to escape and become part of this incredible place.

She would have to shear herself out of her clothes when she got home. That would be worth a paper, at least. *Effects of Cross-Dimensional Travel on Leg Hair and its Interactions with Thermal Underwear.*

She couldn't stop looking around. The first few times she'd portalled in, she'd stayed long enough to test the protection spells on her clothing and take a few initial samples. This time, she'd finally gotten sign-off to stay longer. To go farther into this strange world than anyone had been ever before.

Anyone who'd come out again, anyway.

Everything here was so … so exactly what previous reports of this dimension had been, if you cut out the screaming. Which, despite the peer review process, often made it as far as published work. You'd be reading along, and suddenly the author's dry descriptions of magical currents and air pressure would devolve into *aagh aaaaghhh AAAARRRGHHH*, right there on the page.

The air, if it was air, had a strange colour that shifted between deep-water green and lurid purple; the landscape bulged and lurched and twisted, and seemed to be somehow vastly distant and awkwardly close at the same time, as though the air (was it air?) and the land (was it land?) were changing places, one becoming the other in less time than it took for her to take a breath of what she really hoped *was* air.

Well, she wasn't dead yet.

Anyway, the constantly wobbling landscape wasn't the only thing that had caught her eye.

It would have been lying to say she dragged her eyes away from the pulsing, frond-like growths on the horizon (or were they super close? It was all a bit *Magic School Bus Explores the Digestive System*, regardless). More like she was having to drag her eyes *to* the natural world she was meant to be studying, so she didn't look like a total creep ogling the local who was hanging around near the portal.

She was meant to be studying the landscape, not its inhabitants.

Her ethics approval didn't even cover interactions with locals.

Well, it did. But all it had said was "DANGER! DO NOT INTERACT; IF APPROACHED, RUN" and she'd already ignored half of that by saying hi to her.

And she didn't *look* dangerous.

Okay, so she'd hissed at Sian after she'd said hi, but not in a scary way.

And—

Sian forced herself to stare at an undulating length of the landscape and clenched her fists. And she was *really hot*.

She was pretty sure inhabitants of the Endless Void weren't meant to be hot.

Terrifying, yes. Evil and desirous of nothing more than to wreak havoc on Earth and turn its inhabitants into mindless thralls, yes, yes, she'd read the literature on *that*. Freakishly horrible, etc. Apparently, just looking at them was enough to drive people mad.

Sian didn't *feel* mad.

At least, no more than usual, her usual self being the one who had begged and bothered her department's coven head to let her do her thesis on the Endless Void. The poor woman had probably weighed up the fallout between letting Sian do it and probably ending up dead, and not letting her and dealing with her continued campaign of bothering, and well – here she was.

Getting the hots for a creature from another dimension.

Sian liked to think she had a fairly good grasp of her own attractiveness. She was built like a brick shithouse, tall, and sturdy in all directions, with sun-roughened pale skin and short dark hair. Girls gave her second looks when they saw her from behind. And plenty of them gave her an appreciative third look when she turned around and they saw that her thighs and arse were attached to someone with tits to match.

But that was human dating. Which usually ended badly for her, because it turned out even the most appreciative thigh-lovers got sick of being second fiddle to her obsession with the Endless Dimension.

She glanced sideways. The local – seriously, she had to come up with a better word than that, but the only alternatives from the literature were even worse and she wasn't going to go around referring to her as a 'Godless atrocity of creation', even in her own head – anyway, she was shorter than Sian, mostly humanoid, but with an odd formlessness where the parts of her face and body met. As for her clothing … honestly, Sian wasn't sure whether the nightgown-like shape muffling her body was *actually* clothing or some sort of natural lichenous covering, and she was surprised how much she wanted to find out which it was. The strange woman's skin was a pale purple, and her hair floated around her calm, watchful face like seaweed. And her eyes…

Wow.

She'd probably have to come up with something better than that for her report, but for now, 'wow' would have to do.

Sian weighed up her options. Much like her department coven head, she thought, she could either have another go at it now, or give up and spend the rest of her life yelling at herself about it.

She sidled closer.

"So," she said, casual as. "What brings you here to the Endless whatever?"

The woman stared at her with those big, shimmering eyes.

"Guess I should say what brings me here, eh? Since I'm the one who's, uh, come here."

The woman blinked at her.

"My name's Sian, by the way. Uh. I already told you that, though."

Fark. This was what academia did to you. She couldn't even small talk properly.

The woman's lips parted. She blinked again – and new eyes appeared above and below her existing ones, to blink as well.

Sian couldn't stop her own eyes from going wide. "Wow! Are you – you can – extra eyes – I mean, shit, that's probably really rude to ask about, right?"

Come on, she thought privately. *That's got to do it. Doesn't everyone like a chance to tell someone else they're behaving like a total shit?*

Especially if that someone was her, in her experience.

Oh, God, does this count as negging? Am I negging an alien being?

But the other woman still didn't say anything. Her extra eyes vanished, and her mouth pinched shut. Dark splodges appeared where her eyebrows would be, if she had eyebrows.

Sian's heart sank. "Ah well," she said, trying to sound cheerful for the – shit. The recording! She'd forgotten about it. Very rightly, her research assistant Jonesy had suggested that if the Endless Void did break her mind, an audio recording would be better value than whatever she could remember herself, so she was all wired up and later she'd have to come up with an excuse not to let Jonesy transcribe her failing to flirt with an other-dimensional being. Fan-fucking-tastic.

"Nice to meet you, anyway. But I'd better get on with it, eh," she said, again for the benefit of the bloody tape, and gave the rope attached to her harness three quick tugs. The rope extended back behind her through the portal where, unless something had gone terribly wrong or his latest undergrad booze-up had finally gotten to him, Jonesy was keeping the portal steady until she returned.

The rope twitched in her hands. Three responding tugs from beyond the portal. Jonesy was up to the mark, after all. Good-oh.

Sian unclipped an anchoring rig from her harness and attached it to the most solid-seeming outcrop of … well, not rock, but *something* … her side of the portal. She put all her weight on it to check it would hold fast, then shot one last smile at the purple-skinned woman.

"I'll leave this in your safe hands, shall I?" she declared sunnily and, before she could distract herself by checking whether the woman actually had hands or not – oh, God, what a thought, and one that raised far too many other thoughts – rappelled off the side of the portal.

Trillin watched the human disappear down into the Endless. *Sian.* She watched *Sian* rappel down into the Endless, and all the things she hadn't said to her before she left rolled around in her mind.

Maybe it was worth becoming one with the Endless again, just to have more space to hide from the memory of how completely she'd messed that up.

An added temptation, for the first time: she wouldn't be *her* anymore. The memories wouldn't be about *her* staring at Sian like a mindless fragment while she tried to make conversation with her. That silent, staring weirdo who'd accidentally created herself some extra eyes to stare with would just be a memory of something part of her had once been, and never would be again.

She sagged. She sagged further, and more squishily, than Sian would have with her straight bones and knee joints, and she glanced down at herself to see that her legs had turned into tentacles *again*. Existence eternal, how embarrassing.

She hadn't reckoned on how difficult it would be to keep her new shape while trying to figure out how to speak, let alone what to say.

Whenever she almost got to the point of maybe actually producing the words 'Hello' or 'My name is Trillin', her insides had gone all wibbly. And her outsides, too.

This was *awful*. How did other fractures of the Endless manage it? The last one that Trillin knew of, from a few centuries ago, had entranced dozens of thralls before the humans had driven it back and the Endless had sucked it up again. And she couldn't even manage to *talk* to one?

Not that she wanted to enthral Sian. She wanted … something new. Something she couldn't find memories of any part of the Endless ever being, or having.

But the humans it had encountered had it. A special connection between two or more of them that sometimes helped them to escape the Endless, so that instead of their memories, all the Endless had was the shadow of them slipping out of its clutches. There was one memory in particular the Endless didn't like, at least to the extent it liked or didn't like anything. A woman standing over what remained of a fragment of the Endless right before the whole swallowed it up again, some sort of weapon in her hand, saying over her shoulder to the man behind her, "How's *that* for girlfriend material?"

The Endless might not have liked that memory, but Trillin did.

And she wasn't going to give up. She let her tentacles collapse under her for a few more minutes, then firmly straightened them up with an internal skeletal structure – ankles, she told herself, and knees – and stood up again.

15

She would have another chance to speak to Sian when she came back. Right? Yes. She must be coming back at some point, Trillin reasoned, because she was attached to the rope and the rope was attached to the portal. And when she did come back, Trillin would say … something.

Something really good.

Smart. Witty. Maybe even … alluring.

Trillin wasn't entirely sure what alluring meant, but she suspected it was a big part of being girlfriend material.

She was about to start deciding what smart, witty and/or alluring things she could say to Sian when the part of the Endless the portal stood on began to melt into acidic putrescence. The portal sizzled as magical defences activated.

The rope trailing out of it was shielded, too. But, less than a human's arm-length from the portal, its defences failed. Acid slimed over it, a lick from a mindless tongue, and the rope snapped.

Sian lobbed another fireball at the monster as it charged towards her.

Damn it, this field trip had started off *so well*. If you ignored her failed attempt to chat up the purple woman, which she was absolutely going to ignore and also clip out of the trip recording before anyone else heard it.

Of course, to do that, she'd have to survive this.

What happened to the rope?

She had rappelled down until the glow of the portal was a dim light far above her. The air was thicker down here – still perfectly breathable, thanks to the charms woven into her gear, but *dense*. Some of the supposedly solid ledges and outcrops of rock she tried to balance herself against were disconcertingly permeable. And floating. Basically, the Endless Void dimension equalled weird shit central. Marvellous stuff.

Until her bespelled, enchanted, purportedly unbreakable climbing rope had snapped far above her. No time to wonder why. She'd fallen ten metres to what passed for ground in this dimension.

Fortunately, it was soft. Unfortunately, it immediately attacked her.

Well. Fine. In the interests of full disclosure and not losing her funding when someone noticed holes in her story, it hadn't *immediately* attacked her.

It was a quadruped the size of a Toyota Hilux, seemingly made up entirely of eyeballs and teeth. She'd landed on it approximately where its shoulders would have been, except they were teeth. Teeth that moved and ground beneath her feet so that for a moment she thought she was lunch, until she realised they were moving *away* from her feet. For a moment, she had been standing on craggy skin, then for another, grosser moment she was standing on a red-rimmed eyeball that popped out from the skin and then that, too, slid away

17

towards the front of the creature's head.

It took her another moment to figure out why.

The ute-sized monster was biting at an outcrop of soil and rock. As it tore off pieces, they changed. They didn't fall like rocks should, even taking into account the strangely solid air; they twisted and reshaped themselves and by the time they hit the ground they weren't rocks anymore. They were little creatures. Tumbling, wriggling, scuffling little beasties that looked like what a rabbit might look like if it had forgotten what it was.

And the monster Sian had landed on was eating them.

"Oi!" she'd shouted, and kicked it for good measure. "Pick on something your own size!"

It had. Hence, fireballs.

Sian threw herself sideways as the monster barrelled towards her, using her rope to swing herself wide. She didn't see whether her fireball did anything useful, but she got a face full of muck, and the monster missed her – good enough.

She summoned another fireball and loosed it above the monster's head. A warning shot, she told herself, already sketching out her trip report. A warning shot, not meant to do any damage.

It didn't do any damage at all.

The fireball seemed to forget what it was the moment it left her hand. It glooped in on itself, more liquid than fire; it grew hair, and lumpen limbs, then went all watery; by the time it hit the monster, it looked like a feathery fungal growth.

The monster snuffled at it, and one of its sets of teeth slid up its side to worry it loose.

"Fascinating," Sian whispered, trying to make sense of what she'd just seen. It was as though the changing nature of the world they were in had overwhelmed the spell. And it took a lot to overwhelm one of Sian's fireballs. There was a reason she had been banned from the departmental library.

Following a sudden qualm, she glanced down at herself. She didn't appear to have changed at all; even as the ground shifted beneath her feet, from something that felt like mud, to clinking gravel, to snakeskin smoothness, she remained herself. And the spells in her suit were still functional.

Sian narrowed her eyes at the monster, half wary of another charge, half just inspecting it. It was a changing thing, too, but all on a theme. Teeth. Eyeballs. Dripping, slaggy skin that turned inside-out and revealed more teeth, which made her stomach lurch.

She appreciated that. It was nice to know she still had a stomach and that it could lurch. Point to her; Jonesy had been sure she would be soup by now.

Most of the tiny creatures the big one had scraped out of the landscape had scattered. Sian wondered where they'd gone until she saw one literally get swallowed up by the ground. She gulped.

It made sense. They'd come out of the ground, and they were going back into it. But ... not into holes in the ground. It was as though they were transforming back into the landscape. As though everything here was one giant single organism, and bits could occasionally pop free but were absorbed back into it.

For some reason, she thought of the woman she'd seen near the portal. Was she a part of this ... everything? Would she meld back into the landscape as easily as the rabbit things?

But not all of them were merging back again. One of them was running towards her. If you could call it running. Stumpy legs emerged from its body, hit the ground, and folded back up into its belly, instantly replaced by new legs that kept it tumbling forwards.

It hit Sian's leg and bounced off. She picked it up.

Picking up the local wildlife was definitely not covered in her ethics approval, but she was hardly going to be able to study these things if they all got eaten or dissolved before she got a look in, right? It was a ... sample.

A really cute sample. It was sort of bread-shaped, covered in soft fur and oddly wriggly, as though it hadn't yet decided what it wanted to be. Not like Mr Big and Teeth over there, who was still gnawing on what was left of her ex-fireball.

Not like the purple woman. She seemed certain in her shape, too. Which was human-shaped. And...

Sian frowned. Every time she'd come through the portal, testing its stability and the wards on her clothing and equipment and the whole 'Can I even breathe in here?' question, there'd been something watching her. Something, or someone, almost human-shaped. Oddly wobbly, or lumpy, it hadn't looked the same every time, and Sian had thought that meant it was a different being every time. But maybe…

A roar cut through the air, and Sian swore.

Right. Evidence suggested she was busy getting lost in her own thoughts when she should really be focusing on not dying.

The teeth-monster roared again, eyeballs bursting out from its skin and focusing on her with stomach-churning intensity. Teeth glittered in every inch of space, ready to rip and tear.

This would have been the perfect time to take her bunny monster – uh, sample – and release the emergency recall spell woven into her rope, which would have shot up back through the portal to where Jonesy was waiting and let him know she was ready to come back, pronto.

Instead…

Well, fuck, she thought as the monster hit her dead on. She slammed into the ground a good few metres away and all the air smacked out of her.

Then the huge weight was gone. Sian sucked in a breath that didn't fill as much of her lungs as she had hoped and rolled over just in time to see the monster wheel around.

It stomped its feet angrily. They were tangled in the loops of Sian's rope, and it seemed confused (or maybe just enraged) by the fact the rope was keeping its form. Which the creature promptly dealt with by biting through it.

And Sian hadn't even stood up yet.

She formed another spell in her mind. Fireball. Right, because that had worked so well last time. She let it drop and pulled her magic in another direction.

The landscape here had sucked up the tiny bunny creatures. Maybe it could do the same to the tooth monster.

She focused her magic on the ground. Which was surprisingly difficult. The ground *reacted* to her magic – pulling away, then pushing close, like it wanted to get a closer look. Creepy, but maybe she could use that.

The tooth monster lowered its head. Hundreds of jaws sprouted from it, each one lined with row upon row of shark-like teeth. Sian twisted her magic – and let it go.

The shapeless wave of power rushed towards the monster, and the ground followed it, insatiably hungry.

A tonne of dirt hit the monster like a tsunami.

Sian scrambled to her feet. Barely. She'd put everything into that last rush of magic, and that left her with…

Herself. A big empty gap where her magic wasn't. And her escape rope, her only way home, bitten to pieces.

She took a deep breath. She could replenish her magic. There had to be power here, right? How else would everything in this world keep changing? Sure, she'd prefer to stretch out in her aunt's herb garden, letting the sun and the scents of a hundred green growing things fill her with their strength, but weird goopy-land magic would have to do.

She reached out – and stopped.

Whatever power was in the land here had followed her magic. Followed it like it wanted to *devour* it. Like it was as hungry as the tooth monster.

Maybe ... maybe she didn't want to invite that inside herself.

She groaned and stared at the rope. Maybe, after she'd caught her breath, she could tie the pieces into something long enough to secure herself to the floating rocks and undulating cliff faces and climb back up to the portal. Yes. That sounded like a plan. Since Jonesy wasn't here to tell her it was a fucking stupid plan, she might as well think it was a good one.

She just had to ... catch her breath. In the weird, dense, undulating air.

Sian found a suitable probably-a-rock and collapsed onto it. It oozed slightly beneath her, and she buried her face in her hands.

She had better get started soon. Much more of this waiting and she might have to admit that – that—

She groaned. That there was probably a reason no one had ever found their way back from the Endless Void.

That her supervisor was going to have a Bad Conversation with her family.

That Jonesy was right, and she really should have done more testing with equipment that could instantly broadcast back to Earth, so that at least what she'd seen here might be of some use to future researchers instead of stuck on a memory drive stuck on her corpse for the rest of eternity.

Ugh.

This was why she always jumped straight in. If things went wrong, they tended to go wrong fast, and either she fixed them fast or, she'd always assumed, things went worst-case-scenario fast and then there was no point worrying about it.

She'd always managed to fix things fast in the past.

She'd never expected the worst-case scenario would be so slow.

Or the only fix she could see being so slow either, she reminded herself, because there *was* still a potential fix. Climb back up. You know, just free climb a few hundred metres of constantly moving vertical landscape. Easy.

The ground shifted. Sian lifted her head in time to see the mass of rubble that had swallowed the tooth monster begin to move.

More normal-to-this-dimension changes, she told herself.

Then the monster burst out.

Sian was on her feet before her brain registered more than an *oh fuck*. The tooth monster wasn't dead. It was hugely, screamingly alive, and instead of melting into the rubble as it fought free, the rubble was melting into *it*. Making it bigger.

"Aargh," Sian said, eloquently. She tried to walk backwards and fell over the rock she'd just been sitting on. It sucked experimentally at her boot as the monster shook its head slowly from side to side. Its eyes didn't move at the same speed as the rest of it, but one by one, they all focused on her.

24

"Aargh," Sian said, more quietly.

She was still cradling the bunny creature under one arm. It squeaked as she tucked it into the front of her spellsuit, then stayed still, a warm, trembling weight against her chest.

"All right," she said, clenching her jaw to stop her teeth from chattering as she stared up at the monster. "Let's try this again."

The monster rushed her. She got out of the way – just – but it was bigger this time, and instead of slowing its charge and stopping before it turned, it spun on the spot. Sian was still trying to pull together a plan. She had no magic left, but maybe she could grab the rope, try to tie the thing up or choke it … but how could you choke something that changed its form as easy as breathing? God, she should have taken Jonesy up on his suggestion that she learn how to shoot, and brought along that old shotgun he lifted from his mum's farm—

And then there was no time to think. The monster attacked; Sian ran, and feinted, and tried to get away, but she could already see how this was going to go.

She was getting tired. The monster wasn't.

And this still wasn't as fast an end as she might have hoped for.

She picked up a rock, meaning to use it as a weapon, and it squeaked and wriggled in her grasp. She dropped it, feeling sick. She couldn't use a living thing as a weapon – and not just because the monster would probably just eat it and become even bigger.

All she had left was the rope. She hefted a length of it, as though there was anything useful she could do with it, and the monster reared above her.

Just as she thought everything was over, something plummeted down from the sky and crashed straight into the monster.

She hadn't meant to land *on* the other fragment.

It had been bad enough trying to keep hold of herself as she fell through the Endless. She'd almost lost a limb to a sudden mist of Endless intention, and had fallen tentacle-first into the first whispers of fragmentary thoughts and plans all their own. Her awareness had stretched out, the edges becoming fuzzy as the line between *her* and *all* began to blur. She'd had to hold tight to *her*. As tightly as she was holding on to the end of the rope.

At one point she had bounced off something and it had exploded into a thousand feathered, screaming ribbons. She'd been tempted to absorb some of them – she was still so much smaller than most other things in the Endless – but then she'd fallen past them and it was probably a bad idea, anyway. Even if she was doing the absorbing rather than being absorbed, who knew what else she would pick up from them?

It occurred to her shortly after that she could have created wings for herself instead of just falling, but by then it was too late. She landed directly on the brutish fragment of the Endless that was standing over her human.

And it exploded.

All her tightly held edges splattered at the impact.

Hunger.

The creature she'd exploded into didn't have a mind, as such, but it had wants. It was all want. All consuming, hungering want, to eat and devour and become bigger so it could eat bigger things and become even bigger and even hungrier.

It felt ... familiar.

Like parts of the Endless had been this before.

Like she had. Because all of her had been a part, once, and the part remembered the all.

Trillin struggled to keep herself intact. But there was so much more of *herself*, now that her edges had let in this new matter. The bit of body she'd formed and reformed for herself was barely a nibble in comparison. And that was the only bit of body that was used to holding her mind. Used to keeping her mind what it had been, not—

She had been here a long time. Eating. Finding things to eat. She had been about to eat a small thing, newly scraped from the Endless, and then something bigger and better had come along...

They made eyes and stared out at the human.

Hunger.

They made teeth.

Hunger.

The human stepped back, but – it had done that before, too. They knew how to deal with that. Move faster. Wear it out. More work than the small things but a bigger feast.

Eat—

No!

Something rose up inside them, determined and angry. It wasn't *food.* It wasn't just any human. It was *her* human!

Trillin folded herself into existence. The hunger fell away. The rest of her body did, too, sloughing off the shape that was *hers* and melting back into the Endless.

She looked down at her human, with her own two eyes, which were in her human-shaped head. The head she had spent so long on.

Her human looked back, eyes wide and … somehow starry, although they hadn't changed their colour.

"Wow," Sian breathed. "That's a hell of a trick."

Trillin had her body back. Her human was alive. Now she just had to make some words.

"I … sss…" she began.

Something moved on the human's chest. Her clothing bulged, and something pressed out from beneath the collar. Something furry and soft-looking.

Trillin couldn't help the disappointment that cut through her.

"You changed," she said, and suddenly the words came too easily. "I thought you wouldn't. I've never known anyone who hasn't changed before."

"Changed?" Sian's eyebrows went up. She didn't seem to even notice the new part of herself until it pushed another head out from under her shirt. She tucked her human chin down to look at it. "Oh, this wee guy? No, he's not attached. Shit. I hope not."

She pulled it out and showed Trillin that the furry thing was another fragment, not part of herself succumbing to the Endless.

"Cute, eh? That, uh … the other guy was trying to eat it."

"Cute?"

Trillin stared at the fragment. It was tiny, and fluffy, and had made itself six tentative legs and two furry antennae on top of its head. It had one eye, then three, and settled on six.

It was too small to have a mind of its own. Trillin wondered if it even had desires of its own, like the creature she'd almost absorbed. Or maybe it was just a tiny bundle of fuzz, content to be carried around by its human.

Sian dug her fingers into its furry coat, and Trillin thought for a moment she was trying to absorb it, but the fingers and the fuzzy crumb of Endless stayed distinct. Whole. Touching, but separate.

A new, unpleasant sensation stabbed through her. Why had she made herself so big? Maybe if she'd been as small as the … cute … thing, Sian would—

The crumb stretched into the human's touch and formed a mouth to make a happy trilling sound. It was all Trillin could do not to go all teeth and claws. That was *her* noise!

"How did you do that?" she asked.

"What, giving it a scritch? Everything likes a scritch," Sian said, and added to the crumb, "You're like a cat, aren't you? Or a rabbit. A cat-rabbit. With, uh, lots of eyeballs. Which seems to be a trend, round these parts. Which reminds me of another trend, which is me distracting myself with dumb shit instead of focusing on what's important."

She looked up at Trillin, her eyes suddenly bright and sharp and yet somehow the same as ever. "Thank you," she said, her voice catching. "You just saved my life. Out of nowhere. And I don't know who you are, or why you would do a thing like that, but ... thank you."

Trillin ran through all her borrowed and inherited memories and couldn't find anything to say that didn't make her want to curl herself up into a tiny ball and roll away to safety. She couldn't laugh maniacally at Sian. Or turn herself into a duplicate of Sian and taunt her. Those weren't the right reactions.

"Oh. That's okay," she said, and then, after a few seconds of horrible silence: "My name is Trillin."

"I didn't think anything here had names," Sian said and then groaned and clutched her face in one hand. "Oh, for ... that was awful. I'm sorry. To start with, that should've been any*one* here, and obviously people here have names if *you* have a name, and I just ... there is a reason my supervisor very strongly suggested I run like hell rather than interact with anyone here and maybe it's got more to do with me being the world's worst diplomat than him being worried about me ending up a strange toothy eyeball creature's chew toy." She groaned again. "Which is also … probably … a bad thing to say…"

"But you're right," Trillin said. "The Endless doesn't have a name and fragments usually don't last long enough to have them. I made mine up."

Sian lowered her hand. "It's a very nice name," she said, her lips stretching very slightly.

Trillin felt warm. "And most other fragments would try to eat you," she reassured her.

"Uh, cool. I mean, I do try to give the benefit of the doubt… Fragments?"

"Pieces that break off the Endless. Like me, and…" She gestured towards the crumb in Sian's arm. "And…" There was nothing left of the bigger fragment to gesture at, but Sian understood.

"That big bastard?"

Trillin nodded. "The Endless doesn't want. Not much. Just to be all one thing. But when pieces fall off, they want things – to be more, or stronger, or just to be apart from the Endless as long as they can."

"Sheesh." Sian's eyes flicked from the crumb, to Trillin, to the patch of Endless Trillin was standing on, and – slowly – back up to Trillin. It was amazing, Trillin thought, how her eyes and her face could change so much without changing shape at all. "And which of those do you come under?"

This was another of those moments that seemed to require her to say something smart, witty, or alluring.

What did she want?

"I've been watching you," she said, in the absence of anything that fitted under the headings smart, witty or alluring. To her surprise, Sian grinned.

"Aha," she said. "So I'm not the only creep around here. Good to know. I've been watching you too, or at least I think I have. It was you, wasn't it, at the portal?"

Trillin nodded. She concentrated on the gesture, creating it using an internal skeletal and muscular structure she formed just for the purpose, and then ruined it by sprouting the wings that would have been more useful when she was falling.

Sian stared at her. "Wow."

"I didn't mean to—"

"How can you do that? Everything here is so ... changeable ... and I've seen creatures separate from the landscape and melt back into it, and that big one was all about the teeth and eyeballs, but you can change your form and stay the same? The same person?"

"Changing is easy. It's staying the same that's so hard." She concentrated and pulled the wings back in.

"Why would you want to stay the same?"

Trillin stared. New eyes opened on her forehead, the better to stare with, and she squeezed them shut and away. "Because I—"

She stopped.

She didn't *know* why.

Because Sian didn't change? Because the Endless was all-changing, all the time, and she was a fragment who didn't want to be a part of the Endless anymore?

No. Because humans didn't change, and the only humans she'd ever seen fall in love had fallen in love with other, unchanging humans. How could Sian ever like her if she were as changeable as the rest of the Endless?

"It had better not be on my account." Sian's grin widened. "I like the ways you change."

Heat rose all over Trillin's skin. Her colour changed, deepening, and fine opalescent feathers rose above the warmth.

Sian's eyes were starry again. "Like that," she breathed. She moved closer to Trillin. "Do you—" she began, more hesitantly than Trillin had heard her ever before, "I mean, you say you've been watching me – and you wanted to talk to me up by the portal, didn't you? And you saved my life, and – that was incredible, honestly, and you're – I mean, I've never heard of it happening before, but most of the records we have are more on the death and destruction side of things than anything … anything like…"

A ripple through the Endless interrupted her.

In her arms, the crumb squeaked.

"… Or, on second thoughts, maybe this is a conversation that can wait until I'm standing on slightly more solid ground." Sian moved her feet uncertainly.

"Even if you find more solid ground, it won't stay that way. And …
it won't help." Trillin's body had developed some new organs by itself,
and one of them was twisting.

"Won't help?" Sian shivered and patted the crumb. "What *was*
that? It felt like being in the middle of a muscle cramp. *In* the muscle."

"You're drawing attention." Trillin hadn't intended to change her
voice, but the words came out in a whisper. Bristles poked up from
her shoulders.

"Good attention?"

Trillin didn't think she'd done anything to her face but when Sian
looked at her, her mouth flattened.

"Bad attention," Sian corrected herself. "Shame about my escape
plan." She flicked the length of rope still attached to her harness, then
flinched as the Endless squeezed around them again. "Was kinda
counting on being able to find my way back to the one way out of
here. Even before the bad attention, which … what?"

Trillin felt, undeniably, the eye of her former and future existence
turning towards them both.

"The Endless. It can sense that something is here that doesn't
belong here."

"The Endless? You called it that before. We call this place the
Endless Void. Is it the *Endless's* Void? Is that some sort of entity this
whole dimension is named after? And it's trying to squeeze me out?"

"Not … exactly."

Sian stared at her. "I'm going to need a bit more detail here."

"The Endless *is* this dimension. All of it. Any fragments you see, like me, or your…" She hunted through her memories for small, fluffy things. "… your pet, we're pieces of the Endless."

"Fragments. Pieces that broke off. But you mean that *everything* here is the Endless?"

"Yes, and—"

"So it already knows where I am? There's no escaping it?"

"No, and no. And it's not only you it's after." Sian looked at her sharply and her spines quivered. "It's after me, too. Because I'm not meant to be *me*. Or if I want to be, there should be more of me. Enough that I can leave some of myself behind if I need to, to get away, and still have enough left to be me."

"God, I wish I had time now to dig into this," Sian breathed, eyes shining. "Leave some of yourself behind? We always assumed the beings who came through to Earth were … but you're saying they're all part of one entity? One entity that wants them back? So it couldn't have—"

Water was sprouting from Sian's forehead. She glanced down at something attached to her wrist and wiped her face. The water smeared.

Trillin moved closer to her. "You said you wished you had time now, but you are talking about it, even though you don't have time."

"I am, aren't I?" Sian's voice cracked. "Oh, hell. At least I'm not dissolving." She shot Trillin a look. "Or should that be, at least I'm not dissolving *yet*? Becoming a part of this place?"

Trillin shook her head slowly. "I don't … I don't think that's how it happens," she said. "But we need to go. The Endless is very big, so it's difficult for it to sense exactly where we are. That's why it is—" Another ripple squeezed her edges. "—doing that."

"It's pinpointing our location."

"Finding the pieces of itself that don't move with it. That have our own edges."

"Dissolving might help in that case." Sian raised a hand before Trillin could disagree. "No, obviously not. But…" She thrust the crumb into her satchel and twisted her neck to look up where she'd come. "My magic's still bust, but I might be able to – I don't know, freeze handholds into it, or…"

"I know another way out."

Another way out. Joy to her ears. In the current situation, at least. Taking a wider view, the Endless having an existing portal out of its own dimension to her own world was not exactly great news.

Trillin was leading her through the Endless. Through the single organism that she was walking on and breathing in, and that kept squeezing itself around her, like an oyster trying to worm out a pearl, or whatever it was oysters did.

She couldn't tell how far they were moving. If her feet weren't stepping one in front of the other, she might have thought they weren't moving at all. The Endless kept changing around them and she had no way of locating herself within it.

She had to trust that Trillin was telling her the truth.

And somehow, she did.

"Another portal?" she asked as she leapt across a pit that turned out to be more solid than the 'ground' either side. "Aargh!"

"A small one."

Sian whistled. "And it goes from here to where?"

Wings unfurled from Trillin's back and she hovered over the pit. "Earth."

Sian got the idea she couldn't be any more specific than that. Well, that would just have to be good enough. It wasn't as though she would be able to give directions to any particular spot in the Endless if the situation was reversed, anyway. Second tentacle to the left and straight on till morning.

They kept running, and the pulses of attention grew stronger. Was it her imagination, now she knew they were the work of some massive consciousness, that the pulses felt alive?

She shared her thoughts with Trillin. And her thoughts about oysters. Then explained what an oyster was.

"But instead of spitting us out it wants to make us part of it again," Trillin said.

She didn't like the sound of 'again'.

"Or not again," Trillin mused. "It would be making you a part of it anew. Everything you are, everything you remember, becoming part of it."

Her voice sounded nearer, and Sian turned her head to see – oh, how incredible – Trillin's mouth had actually moved around her head. No need to turn around or anything; just send your mouth a bit closer to the other person's ears. Marvellous. How much she could learn about this place, if she wasn't currently running for her life.

Unfortunately, being so intrigued by *how* Trillin was talking didn't distract her from what she was saying.

"*Everything?*" she asked.

"Memories, hopes, fears…" Trillin's eyes slid around to look at her as she ducked under a strange growth.

"So it would learn about you." Sian's jaw stiffened. From everything Trillin had said so far, that meant that her new friend would be in even more danger.

"It already knows I exist." Trillin's face twisted. *Actually* twisted. All her features spiralled angrily. Sian was so entranced she almost fell over her own feet. "That fragment I splatted back there will remember a bit of me, so the whole will remember now, too. But it'll mostly remember … you."

Suddenly, Trillin spun around. She reached towards Sian, then stopped when her hands were a few inches from her shoulders. Except her fingertips stretched out further even then, as though they were, despite Trillin stopping herself, trying to touch her.

"I won't let it get you," she said. Her face was on the right side, now she'd turned her whole body around, and Sian got the impression she was trying to look human again. "I promise. This is all my fault. If I'd managed to talk to you before you left the portal, maybe you wouldn't have—"

"Jumped headfirst into danger?" Sian snorted. "Not a chance. Best case, you would have realised I'm trouble earlier, and not jumped down after me."

"Not a chance." Trillin seemed to savour the words.

"Really?"

"Really."

"Well." A pleased warmth was spreading through Sian's body. Maybe this wasn't a total bust, after all. "We'd better keep, you know, not getting killed, then."

"Yes!" Trillin hesitated a moment longer, then flowed away. "It's close – just through here…"

Another pulse squeezed Sian's skull as she followed her new … friend. Maybe more than a friend.

Nothing in the ethics approval about that. Not even her supervisor had thought anyone could get on *that* well with the residents of the Endless Void.

She wondered if—

"*Ow.*" Another pulse gripped her. It felt, unpleasantly, like being squeezed by a giant, damp, soft hand. More intense than the previous ones.

A horrible thought struck her.

"You have all the Endless's memories?" she hissed to Trillin as they scrambled up a glutinous hill.

"That's right," Trillin said.

"Including the location of the – *ow* – the way back to Earth?"

Trillin's eyes spun onto the side of her head. She stared at Sian, horrified, then her hair twisted into tendrils that reminded Sian of anemones. "Yes," she whispered.

"If it's seen me through the tooth monster, and seen that I'm human, it can probably guess—"

"We need to move quickly," Trillin gasped.

The pulses came stronger and closer together. They stopped squeezing, and started tugging, pulling at Sian's skin like they were trying to take her apart.

Her vision went fuzzy as Trillin pushed aside a fall of seaweed-like growths.

"We're close," Trillin muttered. "It's – somewhere – there!"

A hole in the world.

If the Endless was everything, pressing close and changing and clinging, then the portal was nothing. It clawed at her eyes, but it was a relief from the Endless' clawing, too.

It was also approximately the size of a car window.

Well, she'd jumped out of her share of car windows. This would be just like being sixteen again.

"I guess this is it," she said. Huddled into her side, the bunny monster squeaked. She scratched it under the chin – or what she was assuming was its chin – and Trillin made a small, protesting noise.

On impulse, she reached out and took Trillin's hand.

Her skin was cool. Not clammy, like the bits of Endless they'd been climbing over, but cool and smooth. Her fingers curved tentatively around Sian's. Sian could feel the bones and thought, suddenly, Trillin *made* those bones.

Trillin made all of herself. She saw me, all those months ago, and wanted to get to know me better – and this is the body she made herself to do that.

A thrill of excitement went through her.

"You're coming with me, aren't you?"

She squeezed Trillin's hand tighter.

Trillin's lips parted. "I…" she began. "I said I would protect you. And I can do that better here. I can distract the Endless, so it loses track of you and where you went…"

"Until it *eats* you and remembers again!" Sian reminded her. "That's a terrible idea! And not just because it involves you *dying!*"

The world pulled at her. She bent over, clutching her forehead as though she could physically hold herself together.

Trillin's fingers tightened around hers, then twisted, turning into thin tentacles that wrapped possessively around her wrist. "It's almost here," she said. "Quickly. You go through—"

"We'll *both* go through. Please. I'm not leaving you here! I—" Sian doubled over again as the Endless focused on her. Her skin felt raw, like an unholy combination of sunburn and road rash. The crumb

41

monster squeaked, and she tucked herself around it protectively.

"Sian?" Trillin's voice sounded like it was coming from a long way away. The world pressed against her, sucking and clammy. She wanted to reply to Trillin, but she didn't dare open her mouth. Or her eyes.

Something clawed at her mind. It got in.

Hello, it said, and Sian screamed.

Strong arms wrapped around her. Something soft brushed against her cheek and she was lifted up. The Endless was still scraping at her, inside and out, but wherever Trillin touched her, it didn't hurt.

The Endless was *here*. There was no more time to argue, no more time to make up for not helping Sian when she could have made a difference. Trillin leapt through the portal.

There was a moment when the Endless almost had her, burning acid through every atom that made her *her*, and then Trillin hit the ground on the other side.

And the ground stayed *exactly where it was*.

"Aargh," she groaned as she discovered how unhelpful bones could be.

"What happened?" Sian gasped from on top of her.

On top of her.

Trillin had touched things before. She had tested her edges against the Endless, feeling it slip and slide and try to cling to the body she made for herself. This was nothing like that.

Sian was warm and heavy, her body a contradiction of soft curves and hard corners. Her chest moved against Trillin's. A hot gasp turned to tiny droplets on the skin of Trillin's neck. One of Sian's hands had landed on one of Trillin's hands and as soon as she noticed, her body created thousands of extra sensory filaments to get as much sensation from the contact as possible.

Her new heart was pounding. Her skin flushed hot.

Above both their heads, the portal pulsed with magic. The Endless's attention poured through, shapeless and inescapable. It scraped at her end to end as though Sian wasn't there, wasn't pressed close and warm against the edges the Endless was trying to suck back into itself.

"Close the portal!" Trillin had never heard her own voice like that before. It jangled out of rhythm with her breathing and her heartbeat. Panic made her shape not her own. Her form twisted out of her own control.

Sian pushed herself up on strong straight arms and glared at the portal. Her jaw moved, solid and determined beneath soft skin. Magic gathered around her.

Trillin was caught between awe at Sian's protectiveness and relief she hadn't looked down and seen how she was falling apart. She clutched desperately for any variation of the shape she had put on for her human.

Stalwart above her, Sian narrowed her eyes. "What *is* this?" she muttered. "No forma, no anchor on this side. How is it even—" She hissed out a breath and shook her head firmly. "Not important. Right now…"

She leapt to her feet and stood between Trillin and the writhing portal. Magic swelled, forming patterns that shaped the world, and Trillin rolled over in time to see the portal twist shut.

"There." Sian angled out her elbows and put her hands on either side of her middle joint. "Easy peasy. Now, where the hell did that thing spit us out…"

The moment stretched out. Sian kept talking, but Trillin didn't hear her.

The Endless was gone. Trillin was alone – separate, herself, and alone.

Her bones turned to liquid. She pulled them back into shape too quickly, and they turned out wrong. While she was trying to remember how ribs worked, she looked around.

The world she'd fallen into was too much for just two eyes to comprehend. More eyeballs sprouted around her head and dotted along her body, building up a full view of the world around her.

Flat. Everything was flat and solid. Everything had edges and all the edges were flat and solid. Even the colours – and there were colours, brown and white and blue and red – were constrained, leaden, still and lumpen within their flat, solid edges.

This was Sian's world. But it was nothing like her. Trillin knew that wasn't how humans worked but there was no way Sian could have sprung from this … straightness. She could not have built her strong limbs and glinting eyes from these lifeless planes.

The thought sent something like panic through her. If Sian was unlike her world, would she prefer Trillin to be more like or more unlike *her* world? Was it the Endless Sian found compelling, or her? If she kept her edges – but what if she didn't keep them, if she *couldn't*, and what if she needed more matter to make more of herself, what if she *lost* some of herself…

But it was still her world. Trillin moved her eyes in unison, trying to connect what she was seeing to her inherited memories of Earth.

Sian had been so confident and excited in the Endless, even when it was trying to kill her. Trillin didn't want to look like she had no idea what to do here in this changeless world.

First, she let her eyes sink down. She was lying on a solid, flat brown surface. It was portioned into straight-edged pieces that stretched out until they met a paler substance that rose up at a right angle.

Sensory filaments prickled from her skin. Neither surface was completely flat, she realised on closer inspection. That should have been a relief. Instead it was even more unnatural. The small grooves in the floor, the dappling of dents in the walls, should have shivered or bubbled or pulsed, not held still as – as—

What was wrong with her? Fragments had been to Earth before, conquering, cruel. But not one of them had reacted to Earth's changelessness like this before.

They weren't struck motionless by the sheer sight of it, or…

Floor, Trillin thought, stolen memories surging inside her. Walls. And further above, the *ceiling*, more brown stripes and forbidding angles.

Nausea roiled in one of her new organs.

She waited, and watched, but nothing moved.

Except her. Her edges were slithering, trying to find something to cling to and be like in this strange, Endless-less dimension. The floor was unnatural but it was, firmly and unchangingly, what it was. Her body tried to be like it, the same way she would find herself blending and mixing with other parts of the Endless.

She couldn't let it. She didn't want to be the floor. If Sian was interested in the floor she wouldn't have come to the Endless.

Somehow that was the thought that gave Trillin the strength to pull herself together. She wrapped her intentions around her form and levered herself up on perfectly jointed legs.

Her head swam. *She* rose, but nothing else did. The world here didn't echo her movements. It didn't observe and react. It all stayed exactly where it was, flat and overbearingly still. She had known that was how it worked, but knowing it was different to experiencing it. To experiencing the world *not* experiencing her in return.

Wasn't this what she had wanted, though?

Well, not exactly.

She turned to Sian. The human woman was still facing away from her, focused on the empty air where the portal had been and running her hands through her hair. Trillin's attention was caught by the twisting motion of the individual hairs. Even if they weren't moving themselves, at least they were *moving*.

"Archway Lecture Theatres?" Sian was muttering. "We're back at the university? These theatres weren't even built the last time there was an incursion. I know everyone jokes about them being cursed, but I thought that was just us..." Her voice turned grim. "Maybe it's a natural portal. Archway's like something out of Escher, anyway, so—"

"Sian?"

Trillin's voice sounded strange. It sounded ... alone. No echoes from nearby outcrops of reality, fragments of the world trying out her voice for their own.

Just her.

"Sorry!" Sian spun around. She didn't even seem to notice how the rest of the world didn't spin with her. Trillin wobbled on feet that suddenly very much wanted to be tentacles. "Classic me, talking shit when I haven't even—"

Her eyes met Trillin's. Her perfect, changing-unchanging eyes.

They went so wide she could see the white parts of her eyeballs all the way around. Another memory surged up and popped in Trillin's mind. She had seen this before.

No. *She* hadn't seen this before. Another fragment of the Endless had. Long ago, on many, many different human faces.

Sian started to scream.

47

There wasn't much in the world that scared Sian.

But the being in front of her wasn't from this world.

Terror unfurled inside her like burning paper. It took everything with it. Reason. Thought. She couldn't even move. Her feet were concreted in place, her body reduced to a skittering heartbeat and the knowledge she was about to die.

There were no words to describe the creature that had appeared behind her. It was humanoid, with purple skin and hair-like tendrils. Colours and textures washed over its skin, one minute peppering it with lavender scales, the next vibrant magenta feathers. And its eyes...

The small part of Sian that still existed behind the fear wondered if she could get a paper out of what the being's eyes looked like. No, not a paper. A poem.

Shattered crystals, each piece reflecting a different horror. Distant galaxies collapsing into one another, heralding the deaths of millions. Long, pale, many-jointed limbs reaching from the ocean floor and crick-crackle wrapping themselves around anchor chains. Flickering somethings at the corner of your eye, the edge of the mirror, slipping sidelong from reflection to reflection.

Sian's throat was hoarse from screaming. The creature in front of her—

Trillin, a small, desperate part of her mind reminded her.

It was *wrong*. Its edges twisted at reality. It was alien and dangerous and *not of this place* and so horrifically unreal it tore at her mind like wet tissue paper. She couldn't look away. She should run, she should—

But it's Trillin, she saved me—

Darkness crept up from the farthest recesses of Sian's mind, twisting and churning as ancient memories that weren't her own were sucked up from the depths. A thousand thousand years of genetic memory screamed at her not to venture past the light of the campfire. That the monster in front of her was dangerous, was not of this world, was *wrong*.

But—

Loud footsteps thudded from somewhere far away. The monster's mouth stretched into a hiss, and it looked behind itself. It muttered something in words Sian couldn't make out and fled. Legs collapsed into tentacles, skin darkening like shadows, and it was gone.

"No!" Sian burst out, but it was too late. The creature was gone.

She dropped to her knees, lungs burning. No. Not *the creature*. Trillin. Trillin was gone.

Fuck. What had happened? She closed her eyes. Her eyelids *ached*. Her whole body had gone rigid with fear and every muscle hurt as adrenaline pounded through her system.

Looking at Trillin back in the Endless hadn't made her do a Marion Crane in *Psycho*. Her changing, fluid shape, her playful inhumanity, hadn't seemed unnatural there. It had been perfectly natural. Perfectly … perfect.

She drew up a memory of how Trillin had looked. *All* the ways she had looked. The memories didn't make her quake in terror, either.

So what the *fuck* had all that screaming been about?

Sian swore and charged towards the door Trillin had disappeared through. Before she reached it, someone called out from behind her.

"What's – Sian? Is that you? Professor! She's here!"

Sian spun around, already knowing who she would see. A bloke about a decade younger and a head shorter than her, spindly-limbed with a dandelion tuft of white-blond hair.

Great.

She mustered a casual nod. "All good, Jonesy?"

"Better now you're back!" he blurted out, then flushed bright red.

Everheart Jones went by a nickname for obvious reasons, one of which was that the weight of a name like *Everheart* seemed liable to make his own heart give out. He was in his first or second year at uni and an old family friend in the way all Dunedin magic users were old family friends, even if they weren't technically on friendly terms. Sian had vague memories of him running around local witch potluck dinners and the like when she was small and he was much smaller. Back then, the position of annoying tag-along had already been filled by her younger sister Flora, though, and he'd never made much of an impact. But now Flora was overseas pretending she didn't have any magic these days, and Jonesy had come into his own.

To an extent.

Right now, he was staring at her with the slightly anxious ready-to-please look that made him perfect as a research assistant and not much good for anything else. Ask him to watch a brewing potion or observe the stability of a summoning and he would watch it faithfully for hours, but taking the initiative? Not his strong point.

For example, he'd just called out to Professor Havers. But the Prof hadn't appeared, and until he did, Jonesy's brain had gone into standby mode.

"Havers still around?" she prompted him.

He jerked. Despite being slightly built, he gave the impression of gangling, with limbs that twitched like they were on strings. "Yes!" Another twitch, which flung his head back over one shoulder. "He's – oh. He's not here. He must be waiting downstairs!"

Sian groaned. "Better get this over with, then."

Jonesy strutted ahead of her as they rounded several corners, walking widdershins around the building. "Do you think it's luck that Archway is so naturally confusing, or something to do with the Department?"

Sian shrugged. The Archway Lecture Theatres were one of the newer buildings on the University of Otago campus. Plonked in between the austere limestone and bluestone of Allen Hall, and the flood-prone 1960s Arts Building, Archway was a striking geometric mess. The huge numbers painted on its concrete exterior walls – one to four, listing the lecture theatres within – were no use once you were actually inside the building. As long as Sian could remember, people had complained about getting lost the moment they stepped inside.

Most of them didn't realise why. Probably because the existence of a magical subterranean research facility magically dug into the ground beneath the building wasn't the sort of thing that sprung to mind when you were wondering why you kept getting turned around and lost in a place.

Jonesy was still talking, but Sian's attention was elsewhere. Was wherever Trillin had gone. And the fact that she didn't know *where* Trillin had gone gnawed at her like, like that other piece of the Endless had tried to do.

What if Trillin had reacted the same way to Earth as Sian reacted to seeing her on Earth? Not that that would necessarily happen; it wasn't like Sian had reacted badly to the sight of her in the Endless. The opposite, really.

She had to go find Trillin and explain – whatever had happened back there. And, to do that, she had to deal with Havers and Jonesy and make sure they didn't suspect she'd brought back a fragment of the Endless with her.

She was even more vaguely aware of Jonesy's voice becoming frustrated at her lack of responses. Nothing she could do about that. Anyway, a bit of emotion that wasn't trembling servitude or trembling concentration would be good for him.

She'd brought back a fragment of the Endless to Earth. Two

fragments. It hadn't really hit her until now.

Two fragments of the Endless, i.e., one of their dimension's greatest enemies, who had frequently tried to destroy their entire world.

Before she could follow that worrying thought any further, Jonesy slowed down until he was walking beside her.

"I thought you were dead!" he hissed. Or as close to hissing as he ever got. Embarrassment got the better of him partway through the sentence and he almost gulped the last few words back into his throat.

Sian was impressed. She raised her eyebrows at him.

"Yeah, well, I thought you checked all my equipment. What happened to the rope? It was meant to be spelled not to break!"

Jonesy pulled his chin in and then thrust it out, turtle-like. "I had to collapse the portal when the Endless started poking bits of itself through! What was I supposed to do?"

Good point. "Warn me?"

"There was no time!" He gulped again.

"Yeah? Enough time for me to almost get eaten, not enough time for you to whip off a quick alert spell?" She punched him good-naturedly in the shoulder as they rounded another corner. "Fair enough. Try to sound a bit more certain about it if someone official asks, though, all right?"

Jonesy's shoulders radiated misery.

Sian placed one hand against a section of the wall. Reality folded. Just for a moment, anyone looking at them from either direction down the corridor would have seen her pushing against one of the lecture theatre doors, but would be unable to tell *which* lecture theatre.

The door she was suddenly leaning on was the same stained wood as the doors to the real lecture theatres, with a smudged brass hand plate and safety glass window. The only thing that made it different from the other doors was that this one had a sheet of paper tacked up to the other side of the window, stopping anyone from looking through.

She hesitated, ears straining.

Trillin was still out there somewhere. Sian didn't want to be toddling back to her supervisor's office to listen to him go on about what a failure her research was. She wanted to be out there, making sure the alien woman who had saved her life wasn't paying for it with her own.

But telling anyone *why* she didn't want to report back on what was, even she had to admit, a fuck-up of colossal proportions, would be the fastest way to put Trillin in danger. Even running off without telling anyone why she was doing a bunk would raise suspicions. Everyone in the department knew her, and they definitely knew what she was like. They would know *something* was up.

And, hey, no one was screaming. That had to be a good sign, right?

With a sigh that she tried to turn into a growl for Jonesy's sake, she pushed through the door.

It opened into empty mist. No floor was visible below, and no ceiling above; just an endless lumpy nothingness, like the sea fog that poured over the hills outside on summer afternoons.

Sian stepped through without thinking about it. She wasn't a bloody fresher; the department's smoke and no-mirrors trick was a novelty that had worn off years ago.

The mist lasted for one stomach-lurching second. Sian blinked. The transport spell to the witching department hidden deep beneath the university usually left her feeling nauseous, but this time, her stomach – although thoroughly lurched – settled almost immediately.

The teleport spell was nothing compared to the everything-lurching of the Endless, she decided. But it was closer to it than anything else around here. Maybe Trillin would like it.

God, she hoped Trillin was okay.

The spell dumped them both out in the Quad, the outdoor courtyard between the buildings of the witching department – except it wasn't really outdoors. The magical part of the university was all underground, the better to keep it secret from non-magical people. It was an old spell, like a pocket universe carved out of God-knew-what, and Sian suspected the department staff who maintained it didn't even know how it had been created.

The witching department looked like a misty echo of the older parts of the campus above. The bluestone and limestone buildings stretching up to the not-sky on either side could have come from the unmagical university above, except instead of ending in tiled rooftops with real sky above, they disappeared into the mists that filled the 'outside' of the magical campus.

Sian had spent hours as an undergrad peering up at the mists, trying to see whether the upper floors moved on the outside as much as it felt like they moved from the inside.

Now, she ignored all of it, heading past the hall of residence that housed the magical students who lived on campus and towards the professors' offices.

Inside the offices, the floorboards were scuffed by generations of magical feet, and the walls and doorframes were scratched with graffiti from the generations of bored students waiting for their lectures to start. Because they were magical, some of the engraved initials and scribbled caricatures held a shiver of enchantment.

Professor Havers' office was down a set of stairs. The lone narrow window in the stairwell looked out on solidly packed dirt, and there were only two doors off the landing at the bottom: Havers' office and the lab Sian had portalled out to the Endless from that morning.

Here we go, she thought, pushing open the first door.

Professor Havers was the sort of witch who preferred to be called a wizard. He was in his early fifties, with piercing but watery eyes and a small, trimmed beard that stank of hair-managing spells. Being glared at by him made Sian feel like she was being attacked by a malfunctioning fountain, so she was glad to see he was bent over a scrying pool.

Jonesy stumbled in after her, almost closing the door on his own arm.

Professor Havers straightened and peered at them both. His eyes glanced over Jonesy and came to rest on her with what she'd come to call the Wise Mentor Stare. It made him look like he had bad hay fever, and she had only ever seen him use it on female students and, occasionally, vending machines.

Assigning Havers as her supervisor had been the coven head's revenge on Sian for bothering her so much, Sian suspected.

He levered himself away from the scrying pool and sat down at his desk. Sian dropped into one of the chairs opposite, letting her pack fall beside her.

It squeaked.

Shit, she thought. She'd forgotten about the *other* fragment she had brought with her out of the Endless.

Professor Havers steepled his fingers. "Well, Miss Finial," he declaimed. "*Talk.*"

"If I'd known this was a social visit, I'd have stopped off to get some biscuits," she retorted. "Anything in particular you want to—"

Her bag squeaked again and she changed course so quickly she was surprised the wheels didn't come off.

"—bring up before I tell you what happened out there?"

Professor Havers looked relieved she was getting to the point. "By all means, continue."

"You don't want to record any of this?" His desk was as clean as it ever got, but she couldn't see any recording spells or, God forbid, good old-fashioned Dictaphones.

"We can discuss that later."

"Sweet. Honestly, there's not much to say. I don't know how much Jonesy will be able to get off my gear…"

She held up the battered equipment. Jonesy passed a hand over it and sighed. "It's no use! The signal was clear enough when you first went in, but everything after the portal closed is unreadable."

Ace. Sian squared her shoulders and dumped the malfunctioning equipment on the desk. "All right. from the top. I encountered another lower order creature of the Endless when I stepped through the portal. It looked humanoid, so I tried to talk to it, but no go. Figure it was just copying my shape, which it must have seen a bunch of times if it's been there each time the portal formed."

Beside her, Jonesy groaned. "That means our data will be skewed! I knew I should have randomised the location parameters…"

"And ended up with me stepping through into a lava pit or something? No thank you. Anyway, it didn't do anything. Maybe it was a sort of plant. I was planning to take a sample on my way back, but…" She shrugged. "See how that turned out. Anyway, I stuck to the script, secured the rope, and rappelled down to a depth of one hundred metres, which put me vertically a hundred metres distant from the portal. Point to you, Jonesy. I was sure I would end up curling back in a spiral or some weird shit like that, but it seems like they have normal gravity same as us. Did the full scan, noted all notable landscape features and local wildlife, of which there appeared to be none until half the bloody hillside shook itself off and turned into a ravening eyeball tooth monster."

Jonesy had pulled a scrolling length of carbon paper from his pocket. He perked up and tapped a section. "That's what it was! The last data that came through from you was a huge increase in ambient magical energy. The baseline in the Endless is high, but this was…" His own energy drained away as swiftly as, Sian imagined, the Endless' energy had swarmed up. "… very high," he mumbled. "I should have used a spell with a higher detection range."

"And then it cut off?"

"And then it cut off."

Sian cracked her knuckles and described her fight against the eyeball monster. She explained how it started by tearing off chunks of the landscape and how the chunks had turned into individual creatures and skirted around the fact that the only reason it had noticed her was that she'd told it to pick on something its own size. Trillin also didn't appear in her version of events. Instead, she made up a fall through a tear in the landscape and a dashing escape through ravenous ravines, ending in her discovering the second portal deeper in the Endless.

"Which was good luck but is also a worry, right? How the hell is there an open portal from the Endless dimension that opens directly above our freaking heads? It's closed for now, but I didn't wait around long enough to see whether it originated in our world or theirs. If something over *there* created it, all they need to do is pop the seal I put on it and it'll be nineteen-hundred-and-whatever all over again."

The professor raised one finger. "I will deal with the portal," he intoned. "You're right. It's a pity your field work didn't go as planned, but the discovery that creatures from the Endless might be working on new ways into our dimension is … troubling."

"That's one word for it."

"We don't want a repeat of 1926, as you say. Or 1873, or…"

"1650," Jonesy interjected enthusiastically. "At least … approximately … based on oral histories."

"Or God knows how many other times before then." Havers pushed himself backwards, tipping his plushly upholstered wooden chair onto its back legs. "You didn't see anything else come through the portal, did you, Miss Finial?"

Sian's pack rustled slightly. "Nope."

Wow, she was being an idiot. Even she could see that. Led around by her – anyway.

But the bunny thing wasn't a threat. Trillin wasn't a threat. It was the other way around. Earth was a threat to both of them…

And so was the Endless.

"Don't bring this to the rest of the coven," Havers was saying. "We'll deal with this ourselves. It was hard enough to get funding for your little jaunts, Finial, without panicking them over a potential incursion. If we can tell them we've *already* prevented another invasion, however, that's another matter. Now, Jonesy…"

Sian did her best to pay attention, but her attention had decided it would be better compensated elsewhere. The Endless was as much a threat to her two ex-Endless pals as Earth was. It wanted to literally consume them … and if it did, it would gain dangerous knowledge about modern-day Earth.

She couldn't tell either of the others here about that, because they would fireball first and ask questions when they got the funding to do a retrospective inquiry. And Trillin would be dead.

She ground her teeth. Trillin. Where was she? Was she okay? Was she safe?

And what the hell happened back upstairs? Why had she been so scared when she looked at her?

All the records talked about the mind-melting terror of seeing a creature from the Endless. Loss of sanity, witnesses left gibbering wrecks, things not meant to be seen by mortal eyes, etc. etc. But 'terror' hadn't been what Sian felt when she first laid eyes on Trillin in her own environment.

It was only when they came back to Earth that gibbering had become not only an option, but the only option.

Maybe the historic descriptions of the Endless creatures' effects on human minds weren't exaggerated. She had thought they were, even before she met Trillin. Her application for permission to travel to the Endless had been based on the argument that the survivors of previous incursions had been exaggerating to make themselves look more impressive. Even after Jonesy made a very compelling case that they weren't, backed up by various primary sources and the fact he couldn't even poke his nose through the portal without practically wetting himself, she'd figured…

She bit back a groan. She'd figured that even if some people *did* go mad when faced with the unknowable, *she* wouldn't. That she was special.

So much for that.

So much for sinking her body against Trillin's, tasting her violet lips and finding out what those tentacles were capable of…

Sian blinked.

She wasn't terrified now, thinking of Trillin. Thinking of her body. Thinking of Trillin and her body. She did it some more, to test.

Same result. Except this time, she had to shuffle awkwardly in her chair before things became too heated.

And she hadn't been terrified right after they came through the portal. She had stood over Trillin, ready to defend her from whatever might follow them through. She'd been electrified with adrenaline, her mind screaming with victory and a thousand theories and ideas as she slammed the portal shut, but it hadn't been screams of terror.

Not until she turned around and looked at Trillin.

An idea began to form in her head.

The other two were still talking over theories. Which meant that Havers was stroking his miniature beard and talking, and Jonesy was nodding hard and occasionally exploding with a well-meaning and instantly regretted "Yes! Exactly!"

She stretched and yawned until her jaw clacked, which had the intended effect of making Havers wince and Jonesy jump.

"Anyway, I'm bushed," she announced. "You two have fun going over all the data. I'm heading home."

"What data? Your feed cut out when the portal collapsed!"

"The data from before that, then. And the bit from after I popped back into the world upstairs." She cracked her knuckles one by one. "Look, you know I don't get all that number-crunching stuff you do. I'm the field girl. I did the field stuff. I've told you everything that happened after the feed cut out." She hoped like hell they believed her. "Now I'm going to sleep until I'm not seeing everything in double. Catch you in the morning."

She slouched off, waving cheerily as Jonesy complained. The last thing she heard before the door shut behind her was the professor reassuring him her absence didn't matter; theory wasn't her strong suit after all, and this was a job for *complex* thought.

Ouch, Sian thought, and filed that away to laugh about later. Or to be angry about. She'd decide which once she'd found Trillin.

Outside – properly outside, back up on the non-magical campus – the sun had dropped. Archway Lecture Theatre cast angular shadows across the ground. Sian searched every shadow, every architectural corner and bike rack, but there was no sign of Trillin.

Worry clenched cold fingers around her heart.

She pulled her pack around to her front and opened it. The

fragment inside looked fine. All in one piece and that piece the same size she remembered from when they were in the Endless. Like someone had mashed together a bunny and a cat, and a loaf of bread, but in a cute way, not a gross way.

If the Fragment was still here, Trillin couldn't have just evaporated. Right?

A cool breeze shivered across the back of her neck.

Right? she told herself again. *She'll be here somewhere. I'll probably figure out exactly where when I start screaming.*

Maybe it was too well-lit here. Trillin was sensible. Probably. Or so Sian assumed, based on – what? A few minutes' acquaintance? The fact that Trillin had gone along with her and saved her life at risk of her own?

Maybe not so sensible. But she would have wanted to hide, right? Which meant she would head for somewhere less well-lit and less…

She looked around, trying to see the campus from the perspective of an alien being who had spent most of their existence as part of an even larger, ever-changing alien being. Too static? All those concrete slab walls and stone pavers. There were dark corners, but they were *corners*. Angular. Strange and unnatural compared to the world she came from.

Another breeze rustled through her hair and made the leaves of a nearby tree hiss. The wind wasn't the only noise. Sian narrowed her eyes.

She followed the breeze and her instincts down the path to the water of Leith. The steep retaining walls that cut down from ground level were as concrete and geometric as Archway, but the water glistened and moved below them like something almost Endless. The walkways were well lit, but the water was dark, and the darkest patches hinted at comforting deepness.

The last week had been wet. The usual two-week-long winter downpour that left the Leith swollen and first-year students wondering whether it was too late to transfer to a less damp tertiary institution. Dangling strands of ivy and other creepers twisted and tugged along the water's edge, tickled by the movement of the water. Tentacle-like. Almost. If you were drunk, or lost your glasses, or ... desperate.

She glanced around. No one else was within calling distance. There were a few straggling figures down towards the student centre, but the recent bad weather and the looming clouds promising more rain on the way kept people from lingering on campus.

No one to hear if she started screaming. Good.

"Trillin?" she called out. "Are you here?"

There was no response. A second later, though, a glimmer of movement caught her eye. A hint of lavender beneath the shadowed surface of the Leith. Terror ripped through her, and she let it take her into a sprint.

Sian ran downstream, past the Arts building, past another bridge, to where the brutal concrete retaining walls gave way to tussock-covered flood banks. She skidded down the bank into the water, boots sliding on loose stones.

Upstream, the water reached mid-calf, slopping over the tops of her boots, tugging at her legs with rain-swollen strength. If anyone saw her—

No one would. She pushed the possibility from her mind. Anyway, people trudging through the Leith were hardly a rare occurrence. If she'd been wearing hi-vis, she might have been a surveying student doing classwork. Without it, she could always pass as a surveying student trying to catch up on classwork after hours.

Or as drunk. It was Monday night; anything was possible.

The Leith ran beneath the walkway between Allen Hall and Archway. The hollow under the road was wreathed in shadows, the sound of water dancing on the air. Some of the shadows were deeper than others. Literally. Sian plunged hip-deep and cast a quick propulsion spell to push herself back to shallower water before the current swept her away.

She slowed down as she approached the bridge and tried to keep an eye on her footing without actually *looking* at the water, in case she saw Trillin.

"Trillin," she whispered as she plodded through the water. "Are you there? Are you okay? I'm sorry I screamed before. I have a theory about that, but…"

The weight of the fragment in the bag butted against her back and she forced herself not to sigh. *But testing my theory is going to be embarrassing and probably horrible*, she added silently.

"… But we'd better get somewhere nobody else is going to interrupt us, first. And I need a drink. And food. And to explain to you what drink and food are, maybe?"

Her voice ran out. She could have hoisted it back into place, but something told her that her usual habit of letting her mouth run wouldn't be the best idea right now, since it usually involved letting her brain dig into its most niche and irrelevant back-alleys.

And right now all those back-alleys were tracing her worries and fears and the possibility this couldn't work, that she'd somehow signed Trillin's death warrant by getting her involved in her own problems. Her own problems like almost getting eaten by Trillin's ex… self… creature.

God, this was all so weird. And usually she loved weird. She loved the *Endless*. Sure, it was dangerous in an extremely deadly way and had scoured Dunedin of almost all its witches at least once in semi-recent history, but it was…

She didn't have words for what it was. Which was good, because if she ever let her mouth run the sorts of words she suspected she *would* use if she did have words for it in front of Havers and the others, she would probably not be allowed to engage with the Endless at all. People would get a bit weird if they realised she didn't just want to find a way to prevent the Endless from ever threatening Earth again, she kind of wanted to bang it, too.

A specific bit of it.

A specific bit of it that she could no longer look at without wanting to scream her head off, and not in a fun way.

"Sian?"

The hairs on the back of her neck went up. In a good way. *Thank God*, Sian thought, and very carefully did not turn around.

"Trillin?"

"Do not worry. I will not go around to the side of you that your eyes are on."

Sian bit back a burst of laughter that had equal chances of coming out relieved, or hysterical. Or possibly as some sort of embarrassing sob. Either way, nope. "Good idea. Not that I'm a great conversationalist at the best of times, but we're never going to get anywhere if I'm busy screaming my head off."

"You were very … loud."

"That's one way of putting it."

"I am sorry."

Because Sian was an idiot, she almost turned around. She clenched her fists and braced against the current. "It's not your fault."

"Isn't it?" Trillin's voice was thin, like the wind sifting through a tree with no leaves left on it. "You're not the first. Most of my memories of this world are of your people screaming or—"

"Or what?" Sian jumped on her moment of hesitation. "Is there a way for me to *not* scream when I see you?"

"You won't like it."

"Right now I'll like anything that saves me from shrieking myself hoarse," she retorted. "First things first though, let's get out of here.

All the most annoying witches in this half of the country hang out under that building there, and if any of them pop out for a moonlit stroll, it'll be … it'll be real bad."

The hairs on the back of her neck rose as a soft splashing sounded behind her. When Trillin spoke again, her voice whispered against her skin. "What shape should I take?"

Sian almost moaned. They had to get back home and she had to hear about this not-screaming option Trillin knew about *now*, because she had other plans for what she wanted to do with her mouth.

"Uhh," she said, stalling for time while her brain pulled itself out of the gutter. "Can you fly? There'll be other people on the streets this time of night even with the weather. If you can get above their line of sight, there's less chance someone will see you and freak out."

"The weather?"

Sian blinked. "You know, the…" She waved her hands upwards.

"Oh." Trillin sighed gently and Sian had to close her eyes and count to ten. "I remember. And I remember a way to … keep out of sight, too."

"Great. Follow me."

Trillin knew what shape she had to make. The problem was, there wasn't enough of her to make it with. The last time, the part of the

Endless that was now a part of her had been massive, a devourer and destroyer even before it broke through to Earth and new hunting grounds. Its form had shadowed the land below, blocking out the sun.

It would have eaten her without even noticing. She shivered.

But perhaps she could make herself bigger, here. She couldn't remember ever doing it before, but...

She stretched out a hopeful tentacle towards one of the solid Earth-fragments. It stayed obstinately itself, the same way the hissing-flowing water had stayed itself, even when she covered herself in it.

And she was worried the edges she had spent so much time refining would dissolve if she changed her shape too much. Not being able to absorb new mass didn't mean she couldn't lose what she already had.

What would happen then? In her world, the lost parts of her body would become part of the Endless again, but here nothing would soak them up. Would they become their own things? Little fragments of her, here in the not-Endless?

What if she became smaller and smaller, fragments of her flaking off until there was nothing of *her* left?

The hunger of the Endless for the pieces of it that got loose suddenly made a lot more sense.

Armed with that unsettling knowledge, Trillin drew herself together and out. Her arms flattened, pulling mass from her ribs and flanks to form long, ribbon-like wings; her head and neck stretched out and her body followed, trunk collapsing, legs thinning out until she was a series of ripples.

The wind caught her. With her body this thin, the air felt solid and permeable at the same time. Almost familiar. Almost like home. She flowed into it, letting its currents waft her into the void that covered this world's impenetrable surface.

Below her, Sian turned around.

"Trillin?"

Trillin opened a new mouth on her underside, then rethought. To make a voice loud enough to reach Sian would risk being overheard by other humans, and she didn't want to give anyone a reason to look up. She stretched out a tendril, fingerbone-thin, and wrapped it around Sian's wrist, carefully out of the human woman's sight.

Sian froze. The only part of her that moved was the steady tick-tick of her pulse against Trillin's tendril. Then:

"There you are," she whispered.

A tremor that had nothing to do with the wind pulsed through Trillin's new body.

Sian wrapped her tendril more firmly around her wrist, and held it close against her, all without looking at it or up into the sky where Trillin was helplessly caught. "I'll show you the way," she murmured.

Trillin did everything she could. She changed the colour of her tendril to match the shades of Sian's wrist and shirt and the crackly growths – trees? – that lined the path. She stayed high up in the wind's caress, billowing her shape so thin it was almost transparent whenever she saw another human.

It was enough. No one saw her. No one raised their eyes to the void and no eyes turned screaming white as the mind behind them broke wide open, ready to be plucked.

No part of the Endless had ever seen the human world like this.

Before, the fragments of the Endless that had sought out Earth had kept all their attention for the humans they were hunting. Even then they had seen little of their prey apart from the cracks in their minds. But what they had seen of the world around those minds was like and unlike what Trillin was seeing now.

It was not as changeless as she had expected. Part of her had feared the whole world would be like the place – the *room* – they had arrived in, flat, pale planes and lines repeating over and over into infinity. But then there had been water, and now there were trees, and surfaces hard and soft, and the chill, caressing wind. And larger, still forms, breaking the world into surface and sky.

The forms were familiar. They featured in her stolen memories, looming large in the background of each fragment's grand plan. Hills, peninsula, harbour, sea. They were the same … and they were different.

No other fragment of the Endless had ever realised this. Earth was not changeless. Its form altered – slowly, yes, but it did change.

The thought comforted her until Sian stopped.

"Here we are," she said, and the *here* made Trillin crumble into a shape the air no longer held aloft.

She pulled limbs and ballooning wings from herself to stop her fall, and landed in a crouch behind Sian. Sian half-turned, then remembered herself and swore.

"Home sweet home. Come on. I'll make you some coffee."

Sian's home sweet home was all sharp angles, but it was softened by thorny fingers reaching up from the ground. Better than the place where they had come through, but still ... unnatural. Un-alive. Was this where Sian came from? This dead place?

Was this where Trillin would have to live, now? There wasn't anything else to be part of here. Nothing to shape herself out of. Just what she'd brought with her from the Endless.

Her body started to unravel.

Back in the Endless, this would be a good time for her to stop being her*self* for a while. To slip back into the totality of unbeing that non-individuality offered. Not the part-her part-other-fragment with its hungering want, but the nothingness of the Endless, a nothing she had not been for so long. Even when she was still experimenting with her edges and had sometimes lost pieces of her body, she'd never let go of that core tangle of memories and thoughts that was *her*. That had a name apart from the Endless.

She followed Sian through a door and a narrow long room and another door, and up a series of right-angles – *stairs*, a memory told her, and a screaming voice from long ago echoed in her ears, *Don't go down the stairs! There's no way out!* But they were going up the stairs, so that was safe, wasn't it? Even if she couldn't quite make her legs work on them and had to ooze back into comfortable tentacles.

Even if Sian liked her tentacles, that felt like failure.

And she probably doesn't like them anymore, anyway, a small, shrinking voice inside her said as they arrived in another room. Humans didn't scream like that at things they liked.

There was enough time for Trillin to worry, and not enough time for her to figure out what to do, and then no time left at all.

Sian stood in the middle of the room, said "Okay, let me just test this theory one more time," and turned around and looked at her.

Her eyes went wide. Her pupils flooded huge and dark and white crept across her cheeks, edging to grey around her eyes and lips. It was the closest to *changing* that Trillin had ever seen the human, and it made her want to turn into a puddle of nothing.

Sian's scream split the air. The filaments on Trillin's head shivered, amplifying the noise and turning it into a cacophony of horror.

Trillin had been wrong about the Endless being nothingness, because some part of Trillin's Endless-memory that had nothing to do with the hungering other fragment said *good*. It said *this is right.* It said *this is the way things work!* It said *Take her, and then others, and then all! Take everything! Be everything!*

Because that was the knowledge the Endless absorbed, over and over again. Every time a piece of it got loose, that piece wanted to be what it had been, but its *own*. To be as big and all-encompassing as the Endless it came from. To consume all.

Eventually, of course, the Endless took back its stray fragments. And, with them, everything they had taken from whatever other

74

dimension they had escaped to.

But that couldn't be Trillin. That wouldn't happen to her.

Because Sian would never be a part of the Endless.

Sian was *hers*.

Even if she was currently scratching her hands against the solid surface – *the door*, a memory told her – she'd closed over the gap in the room when they came in. Her face was turned around on her neck, staring at Trillin. Twisting, changing. *Wrong*.

Trillin pulled herself back into the shape Sian had found appealing back in the Endless. It didn't help. She kept screaming, and in Trillin's mind, other faces twisted in the same way overlaid themselves over Sian's. So many faces, so many shapes and colours and memories.

The Endless couldn't have conquered all of them. Somewhere in her inherited memories must be something to tell her how to make this stop.

Trillin looked around, extra eyes bubbling out of her skin to scan the whole room as quickly as possible. There – another door-surface.

It was almost like sinking into the Endless, the way the door opened and revealed a hidden space within. Unmoving things like emptied humans without heads hung inside it; Trillin tucked herself between them and pulled the door shut behind her.

The screaming stopped.

Some of the hanging things fell down onto her. They were still dead, but Trillin sank down with them, not bothering with joints or bones. Her skin took on the texture of the no-longer-hanging things,

75

and for a moment she could almost convince herself she was settling into a corner of the Endless, somewhere she belonged.

Then her soft changing self bumped against the unmoving surface at the back of the small dark space.

"Trillin?"

Sian's voice was soft, and crackly, and not screaming. Trillin reshaped her ears to hear what was happening on the other side of the door-surface better; footsteps padded gently closer to her, then stopped. Something made a snapping noise, Sian swore under her breath, and then there were two soft thuds and a scrape as she sat down against the other side of the door.

"Sorry about that." Trillin reshaped her ears again, refining the shape until she could hear Sian as clearly as if they were sitting touching one another, with no surfaces between them. "Should have seen that coming. I lost it when I looked at you before. Doesn't take a genius to see that if I looked at you again, it would happen again."

"No, I should have seen it," Trillin argued. "It has happened so many times before."

Sian's voice was strange. "To you?"

"To other fragments of the Endless who have made it to Earth. Whenever humans would see us … them … they would scream and lose control over their higher brain functions. It left space for u … for the Endless to get inside."

"Creepy." Sian's voice was as flat as this world's strange surfaces. "And convenient. How the hell did the Endless manage to find a whole goddamn planet full of people specifically designed to become empty-headed prey animals? That's so – argh! So not what I'm meant to be thinking about right now."

"I thought you might be different," Trillin admitted. "Because you looked at me in the Endless – you looked at *all* the Endless – and you kept your mind."

"Yeah, I thought I was special, too. So much for that theory."

"Is it only me?"

"Shit. There's an idea. One second."

There was a scuffling sound, and a click and *zziiip* sound, and then another scream.

The door opened and something flew through it, hitting Trillin in the chest as the door slammed shut again.

She let herself see in the dark: the *something* was the tiny fragment that Sian rescued earlier.

"Right," Sian panted from the other side of the door. "It's not just you, then."

"Not just me. Any part of the Endless terrifies you now."

"Well it bloody shouldn't. What's changed since we were in the Endless?"

"We're not in the Endless anymore."

"It's—" Sian said a number of other words Trillin didn't catch, very quickly and angrily. "It can't be that simple. Can it?"

Trillin hunted through her memories. "No human has ever willingly set foot in the Endless before," she said out loud. "By the time any other humans were taken there, they had already given up most of who they'd been to the Endless."

"What do you mean by that?"

Trillin paused. A new sensation was flooding her body. Was it ... embarrassment?

Was she embarrassed the Endless had taken over the minds and stripped the lives from so many of Sian's people? And if she was ... was that the correct feeling? Should she be feeling something else, instead?

It was all so hard. The Endless wouldn't have felt anything, but she wasn't the Endless anymore. And she wanted to be the right sort of person for Sian, with the right sort of feelings.

"I mean," she began haltingly, "that when a fragment of the Endless encounters humans usually, it, er, consumes their minds and their memories. Sometimes, the Endless takes back that fragment while part of it is still inside the human, so the human comes too. And they are. Er."

Faces flashed up in her mind of the humans this had happened to.

"They are also usually screaming," she concluded.

"Oh, I knew all about *that*." Sian didn't sound as though she thought Trillin had had the wrong feelings about all the consuming. "We've got records of that sort of thing too. No one ever came back, though I expect even if they had, they wouldn't have been able to add much to the narrative. Not much that made sense, at least."

Looking back on her memories, and those of the consumed

humans before the Endless took them over completely, Trillin had to agree.

"Maybe it *is* environmental." Sian's voice was thoughtful. "Maybe, seeing you and talking with you in your own world – no mind-breaking freak outs – seeing you here, in *my* world … mind go boom."

She paused.

"Shit."

"But that means…" Trillin's voice was small, which didn't make sense, because her vocal apparatus was the same size it had been during the rest of their conversation.

"It means we're going to find a way to change that." Sian's voice wasn't small. Sian's voice sounded like it could charge down the fragment that almost ate her earlier, and the rest of the Endless, and then look for something else to fight. "Because there's no way in hell I'm never going to look at you without screaming again. You risked everything to get me back here safe. I'm not going to let you down now."

Having a theory was one thing. As Havers said – not her strong point. Experiments, though. Sian had always been good at smashing various combinations of things together and calling it science.

The first lot of experiments were largely a failure. Unless she cheated a bit and said she was also experimenting with strengthening her soundproofing charms. It was a good thing her aunt, who had raised her, and whose house this technically was, was out of town. Constant terrified screaming was a bit much even by Sian's usual standards.

Call it experimenting with exercising my voice, she told herself. And seeing how elevated her heartbeat could get without her heart literally exploding in her chest. If you did that, then by the following lunchtime Sian had plenty of data.

Just no luck looking at Trillin without her brain trying to crawl out of her ears.

No luck being a good host, either, even without the screaming. Forget kissing her, even though kissing Trillin was always on Sian's mind; she couldn't even *feed* the woman who'd saved her life. Which was worrying. Trillin had to be expending energy by the bucketload with all her transformations. What would happen when she ran out?

"I will try again," Trillin said, after Sian showed her another video of the human digestive system.

They were sitting together in Sian's room. She'd tempted Trillin out of the wardrobe by promising not to look at her or the tiny fragment, which they were calling Bunny.

Bunny was also spending most of its time in the wardrobe, in a nest made of half a dozen of Sian's old sweaters. It had ventured out, once or twice, wearing her satchel as a sort of turtle shell. She supposed that was as close as it was going to get to being absorbed back into the landscape, like those other fragments had been.

Sian was perfectly happy to keep experimenting with looking at Trillin, trying to figure out a way to stop the madness taking over, but she had to admit Trillin had a point. She was starting to feel twitchy even when she *didn't* look at her. Heck, even looking at her satchel made the hairs on her neck stand up, and she'd had that old thing for years.

Right now she was glaring at the jug, waiting for it to boil. Sian was a coffee person normally, but some things called for tea. Trillin's attention was like the brush of an anemone against the back of her neck. Except *she* was the anemone, not Trillin. If she had whatever it was anemones had – Fronds? Tentacles? – they would have been shrinking back.

Not out of fear. As soon as she stopped actually looking at Trillin, the bone-trembling fear disappeared, which if the response was some sort of instinctual survival mechanism made it a pretty shit one. What was the point of a get-the-fuck-out gene if it turned off the moment you lost sight of what sparked it off? Even when – and this was the bit that made Sian want to find this particular bit of her biological makeup and shake it hard – what she *really* wanted was a get-the-fuck-*in* gene, hahaha.

Yep.

Definitely losing it.

That wasn't even a good pun, fucksake.

She made the grumpiest pot of tea ever, plonked a handful of biscuits on a plate, and sat back down on the floor, all without looking where she wanted to look the most. "Here," she said – ungraciously, and with immediate regret – and pushed Trillin's cup of tea behind her. "Let's try with this. You can dunk the biscuits in it and they dissolve a bit. I thought you might like that."

Or, you know, they would remind Trillin of how the Endless wanted to dissolve her back into itself. She winced.

"Thank you." There was a soft scraping sound as Trillin picked up the mug. Sian pulled up her knees and dropped her head onto them.

"It'll be hot. I don't know if you're sensitive to temperature or not, but just in case—"

"Argh!" Trillin's shriek cut off mid-breath and Sian couldn't stop herself, she turned around and into a searing moment of pure fear. Like staring into the sun and the sun staring back, reaching with burning hands.

Then Trillin's hand was over her eyes. Her fingers split and meshed together, pressing her eyelids shut and sealing them that way, hot and damp over icy sweat. And it shouldn't have worked. But it did.

Sian let out a breath that took her whole soul with it and offered it up on the plate beside the biscuits.

"Trillin—"

"Bunny ate the tea," Trillin said mournfully.

"Forget the tea." Sian's voice vibrated with excitement. "I – wait. *Actually* ate the tea? It's not just, I don't know, gooped up inside it?"

"Yes."

"How? Argh. You can't ask it, can you?" Trillin had explained Bunny didn't have a mind of its own in the same way she did; it was too small.

"I don't need to ask it. I can take the knowledge with a piece of it." A short hiss of breath. "But I don't *want* to."

"What about trading it?"

Trillin made a soft humming noise. It seemed to come, not from her mouth, but all over her body. The tentacle-hand over Sian's eyes buzzed.

"A piece of me for a piece of it. No fragment of the Endless has ever tried that before."

First time for everything, Sian thought. Like being a fragment of the Endless Void that *didn't* want to take and devour everything in its path. Trillin shouldn't exist. She was the opposite of everything the Endless represented.

Sian had to find a way to make this world safe for her. She *had* to. It wasn't just about kissing. She couldn't reward Trillin giving up her whole life by trapping her in a world where she couldn't even go outside without causing a riot.

"*There.*" Trillin's voice was breathy with satisfaction, which did entirely expected things to Sian's pulse. "Now I can eat. Bunny used its suckers, but I think I will use my mouth."

"What did you give Bunny in return?"

Trillin shrugged, or Sian assumed she did from the movement that willowed through her tentacle-hand. "I'm not sure. Some thinking, perhaps. It wasn't much more than movement and hiding before."

And now it was something else. A shiver of witchy excitement joined Sian's various other excited shivers.

"Great. You can eat now, so I can stop worrying about you draining all your energy and not replenishing it. And you're touching me and I'm not screaming." She paused, her heart in her throat. "You realise that, right? We've made a breakthrough. I can't think why we didn't try this before. It makes perfect sense. I don't have to *see* you to ... interact with you."

The tentacle-hand over her eyes changed texture. Tiny fronds ventured out, exploring more of her face. Sian held her breath. Trillin's touch was tentative, shy, and the most incredible thing she'd ever experienced.

"I can't believe we wasted all this time trying to figure out *looking*," she groaned. "We could have—"

Her voice broke off as more exploring tendrils found her skin. Trillin must have given up on being entirely human-shaped; the touches were coming from too many places, tiny effervescent caresses, tantalisingly gentle.

"I won't eat you." Trillin's voice was so sincere, so earnest, that Sian had to bite back a burst of giggles. "I know how to, now, but I won't. I want you to know that."

"I think that's the most romantic thing anyone's ever told me." She tried to make her voice match Trillin's in seriousness, but the giggles broke through.

"I won't eat anyone else, either. I promise. Just tea and biscuits."

Sian was about to tell Trillin that there was more to eat in her dimension than just tea and biscuits – or maybe she wasn't, maybe she was about to tell her something that had nothing to do with that sort of eating at all – when a communication spell blared into life somewhere in her room.

Trillin pulled away and she heard the click of the wardrobe door. Swearing, Sian jumped to her feet. Her phone was streaming acid-green sparks.

Havers. No one else made their comms spells quite so flammable, or sent them directly to *very expensive electronics.*

"What?" she growled as she activated the spell before it could set fire to her desk, her phone and everything else in reach.

"Our young assistant has discovered possible signs of another incursion from the Endless Void into our realm."

She had to hand it to Professor Havers. Even with the threat of destruction looming over them, he managed to hand off responsibility for the potential apocalypse to an underling. If the threat was real, Jonesy should have found it sooner; if it wasn't, he shouldn't have jumped to conclusions so quickly.

"Shit," she said out loud.

"Quite." Havers sniffed. "I expect you're recovered enough to—"

"Yeah, yeah. On my way."

"I should hope so. But don't spread the word. We don't want people to panic unnecessarily."

Dealing with Havers and Jonesy took the rest of the evening. Jonesy had found traces of Endless biological material around the Archway Lecture Theatres. The thought of Trillin losing pieces of herself as she fled from Sian's screaming horror made her chest clench. But there was no sign of anything other than the traces, and they were easily explainable as leftover from the portal, which was still firmly closed.

But not actually *removed*. Removing portals was a bit beyond her abilities, but certainly within Professor Havers'. The fact he'd left it was more proof of what Sian had long suspected: that witches, here in Dunedin at least, were absolutely bonkers. Whatever concern Havers had about a potential incursion of the Endless into Earth was more about the possibility it would reflect badly on his position in the department than because of the actual danger.

It was the same all over the city. It didn't matter whether or not witches were associated with the university, they were all determinedly poor at self-care.

Take the Blackthorns, ostensibly a respected old Dunedin witching family. Half of them either died horribly or cursed themselves into new and terrible forms before the age of forty, and no one batted an eye. One of her classmates in second year had either discovered she had mermaid heritage or been eaten by a mermaid; either way, she'd disappeared, and people just went on as normal. Sian's own parents had both died in mysterious circumstances when she was a teenager. A car crash, apparently, and she still wasn't sure whether she wouldn't have preferred them to blow themselves up with some incredible spell.

Was it any wonder she ended up in this situation, really?

"If anyone asks, we're shutting down the portals for routine maintenance," Havers huffed when they'd cleaned away all the signs of Endless matter.

"So that's it for their research project?"

Havers waved her away. "Don't worry. We'll find something else to do with your funding, before the others snatch it up."

And that, she hoped, was that. Sian raced back up the hill to her little house wrapped up in rosebushes, and only barely remembered to close her eyes as she entered her bedroom.

"We're still safe," she said. "They have no idea you're here. You or Bunny."

"But that's the thing." Trillin's voice wavered. "Bunny's gone."

The tiny fragment had disappeared a few hours after Sian left. "I should never have let it eat the tea," Trillin fretted. "It kept trying to eat other things that I was sure it shouldn't—" She guided Sian's face to look in a particular direction and then retracted her tentacle, and Sian opened her eyes to see a series of perfectly round holes drilled in her desk and the notebooks stacked on top of it. "And then, I think because I wouldn't let it eat anything here, it created a portal back to the Endless!"

Sian ran her hands through her hair. "A portal? How did it make a *portal?*"

"I don't know! *I* don't know how to make portals, and it shouldn't know anything that I don't."

Sian went over to her desk. Bunny had bitten holes right through all the notebooks she'd been using for her current research.

All the stuff about – oh – *making portals to the Endless.*

She dragged her hands down her face and told Trillin. "Can it do that? Learn from eating books?"

"We normally learn from eating each other," Trillin said softly.

"And now it can make portals. That's incredible. I hate it. Where is the portal?"

Another tentacle tugged at her wrist, directing her to look under the bed. "Shit."

"If the Endless devours it—"

Then the Endless will not only know where we are, but it'll also know how to find us. And if it can't fit through that portal, it'll know how to make bigger ones.

She swallowed.

"That's not our only problem. My supervisor is scrying for portals to shut down. If he senses this one, he'll be here in a flash, and if they find you, who knows what they'll do."

"Probably try to kill me in a variety of ways," Trillin said quietly.

"Well, I don't want that to happen!"

"Neither do I. I remember past fragments being defeated, but not killed. But there are … missing pieces. Which means you must have ways of killing us – it – and they must be effective, because not even a little bit of the Endless they killed came back to add its memories to the whole."

We do have ways of killing you, Sian thought miserably. The first part of her research on the Endless had focused on what to do if their activities attracted the attention of one of the greatest threats to Earth. Human magic users had managed to fight back the last incursions, but at great cost. The spell the witches used had destroyed the invasive outcrop of the Endless – and obliterated the humans who cast it.

She thought of the folded piece of the world in the Northern Cemetery, where the victims of the last incursion were buried. Jonesy and Havers might be irritating, but she didn't want to see them blasted out of existence. Who would do her data analysis then?

And Trillin...

She didn't want Trillin to be dead, either. But an unfamiliar feeling jolted inside her. Guilt. This was all her fault, wasn't it? She was the one who had flirted with Trillin every time she went to the Endless. She was the one who had inspired Trillin to put on a human form, and she was the one who had got herself into hot water and needed Trillin to pull her out of it. If it wasn't for her, Trillin would be safe back in the Endless, not here, risking extermination.

And what about the risk she had taken in communicating with part of the Endless? Every witch who knew about their neighbour dimension knew what a bad idea that was. And now she knew *why*. Any new piece of knowledge became part of the Endless's arsenal of tricks against Earth as soon as the outcrop returned to the whole.

What if Trillin returned to the Endless? How would it use what Sian had taught her against her world?

Trillin seemed to be thinking along the same lines. But she'd come to an entirely different conclusion.

"If there is no other way, you should let them kill me."

"What? No!"

"It's the only way to keep everything I've learnt safe from the Endless."

"There has to be another way."

"It has to be death. You can't let them banish me." The tentacle around her wrist tightened. "I can't go back there. The Endless will be looking for me. It wants me back."

"But—" Sian shook herself. "They have to catch you first. Come on. Let's go."

Not out the front door. The neighbours would be home by now and might notice Sian fleeing with a purple tentacle woman in tow.

"Follow me." Sian wrapped her other hand over Trillin's tentacle on her wrist and showed her the back route out of her room, via a window and convenient tree. It was a classic for a reason and had seen her through years of midnight escapades. She liked to think the tree and she had grown up together, a symbiotic relationship.

Sian jumped and clambered down, then turned to warn Trillin of the tricksy branch and the piece of wall that looked solid but was actually an illusion dating back to a particularly drunk attempt to scale the wall a few years back. She got a glimpse of lavender tentacles, little more than shadows, and horror whited out her brain.

Soft tentacles covered her mouth and eyes before she could scream. Her shoulders slumped with relief. "Sorry. Stupid of me," she muttered when Trillin released her.

The night was cool and dark. A sliver of moon hung overhead, more decoration than light. As they moved away from the house, the darkness pulled in.

"I don't know how much time we have, but we need to get you somewhere you can hide." She filled Trillin in on the pieces of Endless that Havers had found near Archway, and Trillin rattled with agitation.

"Did he kill them?"

"What, the scraps he found? Why would he – oh, shit."

"You must!" There was the sound of agitated movement behind her. "I don't think I lost any of myself, but what if I did? What if they are pieces of me and know where I am? What if they are pieces of me *and* pieces of the Endless, and soon both will know, and—"

Panic was a new look for Trillin. Sian reached behind herself. "Take my hand."

The hand that took hers was cool and soft, bones tremulous under skin that was just learning how to be.

"Don't worry. You looked after me while I was in the Endless, and now it's my turn to look after you."

"Even if you have to kill me."

"Yeah, not going to come to that. Let's focus on getting rid of those remnant pieces and getting you somewhere safe first." She gently squeezed Trillin's hand and started walking towards the back shed. "We need to go somewhere there's enough background magic to disrupt the spells my colleagues can use to track your Endless … ness. Luckily, given the number of previous incursions here, the background magic is plenty crunchy, so – what was that?"

That was a fizzing, crackling hole in the air between her and the garden shed. Sian readied a fireball by instinct before remembering how dry the grass was underneath her feet and exchanging it for a telekinetic slap.

The portal was the same static nothing as the one that had brought them back to Earth. A shadow appeared in it, then a shape.

"Bunny?" Sian gasped. "Oh, hell – it's going to let the Endless in!"

It was the perfect moment for Havers and Jonesy to arrive so, of course, they did.

Havers' car was an excellent loophole for not getting stuck in traffic. It teleported itself place to place in the time it would take you to drive there anyway, but without having to navigate around other people on the road. Sian had watched Havers spend the larger part of a journey lingering over his coffee in his office before suddenly realising traffic had eased and he had to run to the car to get inside before it vanished.

The driveway was just visible around the side of the house and, with it, the growing shadow of Havers' car.

"Hide in the shed. I'll hold them off." Sian squeezed Trillin's hand, wishing she could look at her.

Trillin's hand slithered out of hers. There was a sound she hoped was the shed door opening, then closing.

Sian slowed from a sprint to a saunter as she rounded the corner and watched Havers' car finally clunk into solid being. Havers and Jonesy got out of the car, and Sian's eyes snapped immediately to the satchel over Jonesy's shoulder. He'd stored the Endless samples in there earlier. What were the chances they were still there?

Given Havers' dislike of anyone else knowing what they were doing, and the way Jonesy was acting like the bag might explode at any moment, she was guessing *high*.

Havers glared at her. "You're alive? Good. Something's happening. I—"

"Portal opened in my bedroom, yeah."

"You're already aware?"

"Why do you think I'm down here?"

"Professor, the samples are pulling towards something." Jonesy was fighting with the satchel now. Something inside it thudded in his grasp, yanking him towards Sian. Her breath caught. Was it pulling in the direction of the shed – or her? "Shouldn't we begin preparations for the razing spell?"

The one sure-fire way to destroy the Endless. And possibly them with it. Sian's skin chilled.

Havers waved Jonesy's pleas away. "Not necessary. You know how flashy a spell like that is. Think of the effects on our research! Not to mention we'd have to explain – ah."

It wasn't a satisfied *ah*. Sian turned, fearing what she would see.

Another portal fizzed into existence. Then another, then another, a patchwork of static tearing apart the space between Sian and Trillin.

Her heart sank.

The Endless was coming for them both.

Trillin watched from gaps in the small building's bones. The same frond-like, thorned *plants* from the main house grew thickly around the shed, twining around and piercing through the gaps in the walls; they almost moved enough, in the slight breeze, for her to feel comfortable among them.

Better than comfort, they offered cover.

She dropped to the floor, oozed herself flat and many-headed, and wrapped eyestalks around the thorny bushes to see what was happening outside.

What was Bunny doing? It was going to destroy this for both of them. She didn't understand. She was sure the fluffy fragment wasn't like her – it was like the fragment that tried to eat it, a cluster of instinct and longing, with none of the cunning that larger fragments acquired. There wasn't *enough* of it to have thoughts that big.

Yes, she had exchanged some of herself with it to gain the ability to eat this world's food, but surely not that much. And how was it managing to create these portals, and target her and Sian with them?

Was the Endless controlling it?

Her tendrils curled inwards. There were dozens of tiny portals now, and Bunny briefly appeared in each as they were created. She only caught a glimpse of its face each time. Not enough to know if it truly *was* the little fragment that had come to Earth with them.

It had been back in the Endless for hours now. It might have been reabsorbed by the whole and what she saw like one of her eye-stalks extending out of the Endless. A fragment-stalk. A trick.

She knew about tricks. The *Endless* knew about tricks. About tempting limbs waving over magical trenches that turned out to be constructions wrapped in human clothing, and bright, alluring shapes that turned out to be only illusions projected upon more clothing-stuff. Humans had tricked the Endless many times before. Perhaps it wanted to trick them in return.

"I let you eat my tea!" she whispered to the next portal that appeared. The Bunny-shadow inside it looked at her.

"Sweek!"

Outside, someone shouted. Trillin swivelled all her eye-stalks around, but it wasn't Sian. It was another human, with long gangling limbs. He was carrying something that wanted her with a hunger she could taste, all over her skin.

The Endless. They'd brought it here.

"Sweek!"

Bunny darted out of the portal. Terror rolled off it. It had gone back to the Endless and escaped – but now the Endless had followed it back to Earth.

Trillin quailed as the entity she had once been part of pushed at the dozen tiny holes in the world, trying to force its way through. It might not know how to make its own portals, yet, but it would take advantage of the ones Bunny had created in its panic.

There were so many lost fragments gathered here together, and the Endless wanted them all so much.

Reality cracked. Splinters formed between the portals. Sian's edges grasped at the world around her, holding it so tight pieces fell off. She wanted to hide, like Bunny had hidden all day, in its soft, dark nest. The cracks between the portals widened, until the air between Sian and Trillin was more portal than Earth.

"Stop it!" someone shouted. "If it goes the whole way around it'll form a megaportal. We'll lose whatever's inside!"

"My car!" someone else roared.

Sian was inside it. Couldn't they see that? Sian, a flicker of dark hair and pale face and determination in the gaps between the sizzling nothingness, heading for the gangling human. Towards his fragments of Endless. Trillin's organs, the ones she had made for eating with, all hurt.

The older human male raised his hands, calling magic out of the air itself.

It wouldn't be enough. Whatever he was doing, it wouldn't be enough.

Or it would be too much, and Trillin didn't know which was worse.

She flowed through the gaps between the building and the thorny vines that were slowly devouring it. Bunny caught sight of her. All its features surged to her side of its body as it ran to her, caterpillar legs tripping it up. She whisked it up with one tentacle and held it close. Its edges were unravelling with terror.

Her own edges hummed. It was all she could do to keep herself together. "Sian!" she called from a hundred desperate mouths.

All three humans stared at her. Horror bracketed their minds. The Endless reached for its lost fragments, a hundred tentacles striving, wanting, but it wasn't going to let this other feast get away. It reached for the humans as well.

The older man's magic spiralled out of control. It met the splintering portals and pulsed, and suddenly Trillin knew what spell he'd been trying to cast. Destruction, so total it would carve half this hillside from existence and take them all with it. Earth would be safe. There would be no portals anymore. No way in for the hungering Endless.

No her. No Sian.

The portals cracked together, fusing into a single raw open mouth with a sound like the end of all worlds. White light filled and overfilled Trillin's senses. Just for a moment, she was out of Sian's sight.

Sian swore loudly in the silence left by the tearing between dimensions. She raised her hands and the spiralling magic twisted up and around the portal, but it wouldn't be enough.

Bunny knew how to open portals. Maybe it could close portals, too, and that was knowledge she needed. Even thinking it felt like a betrayal of everything Trillin had made herself become, but what else could she do?

Her edges frayed. Bunny's edges frayed, too, and that made it easier until suddenly it all went wrong, and she wasn't Trillin-using-Bunny's-knowledge, she was—

Hide. They needed to hide. They were a too-much something here, and a too-much of anything got eaten. They needed to get away. They had tried to run and hide in the place they remembered, where they had come from, but everything there had wanted to eat them. So they had run back here, but so had everything. And now the world was all too open with too many openings for the everything to come through and although part of them remembered being big and powerful and devouring, right now they were very, very small, and the best thing to do was run and hide.

Though … less small than they had been, and this new part of them was a mass of complexities. The new part of them banged up against the being small and scared and having to run away, and hide

hide hide they needed to stop what was happening hide hide hide protect Sian, protect Sian's world without dying because Sian didn't want her to die and they didn't want to die, either. The Endless had no memories of dying and they didn't want to die here and be eaten and give it that memory and all their memories of Sian, everything they knew about her, everything they had to keep secret from the Endless or it would use the knowledge to hurt her and her world.

They wanted hide hide hide oh they wanted hide hide Sian safe the world safe them safe hide hide wanted hide wanted anything but Sian unable to look at them, them unable to see the stars and wonder in her eyes, unable to touch without the threat of fear, wanted – hide—

The knowledge was right there, and the need. How to create a portal and how to keep Sian safe and their own heart intact.

They twisted the space between worlds around them as destruction spiralled from Sian's hands. Sian's spell razed everything it touched. The fragments of the Endless this side of the portal, the tentacles grasping to tear the world to pieces. Even the portal itself. The part of *them* that had been Trillin understood suddenly what had happened to the fragments of the Endless that had never returned to the whole. This was the humans' defence: this spell that destroyed everything in its radius, even the human casting it.

Sian. No.

The Endless was gone. Its portal had been obliterated and the pieces of it that had made it through were dust. But the spell hadn't run its course yet. It turned back on Sian and the other humans.

No!

They reached out with sweeping lissom arms and grabbed hold of the spell's power like taking lightning into their hands, and shook it out into something new. Not a portal to the Endless this time but a portal to somewhere new, a somewhere to hide and be safe and be free—

Trillin had shucked off the tooth-monster in the Endless, but this was her first experience of being the one who was stripped off like ill-fitting clothing. She fell into herself as the world cracked around her, finding her own edges again with nothing but a faint suggestion that being as complex inside as she was didn't really appeal to Bunny.

Then she was herself again, and the world closed around her.

"What happened?" Sian gasped from beneath her.

Beneath her.

Trillin propped herself up on her limbs, firming them up enough to take her weight. Sian was sprawled beneath her, blinking as though she'd forgotten how her eyes were meant to work.

Her gaze focused on Trillin. Then flicked, ever so slightly, up and down, meeting all six of her eyes.

"Hey," Sian said softly, and smiled. "This is nice."

"You're not scared?" Scared was so small a word for what Sian had been every time she looked at Trillin back on Earth. So much smaller than the feeling welling inside Trillin now at the sight of her human smiling at her.

"Scared of whatever the fuck we just did, maybe, but not…" She lifted a hand and cupped Trillin's face. Longing tendrils crept from Trillin's skin and wrapped around her fingers, unwilling to let her go. "Not you. Not … here. Where is here, again?"

"I do not know."

Trillin raised her head. They were in some sort of structure, with tall, vertical walls all around curving to a peak above. The walls were a pale colour except for partway up, where they became thin and multi-coloured. The colours shimmered and for a moment Trillin thought they were still in the Endless, after all, and this was some sort of trap – the sort of trap previous fragments had set for the humans they were trying to ensnare – before she realised the shimmering was the result of something *behind* the colours.

She stretched her eyes up. Beyond the shimmering was a haze like the split nothing of a portal. A sinuous, here-not-here existence. Things moved but did not seem to notice them.

"Are we underwater?" Sian asked. "Is this some sort of … submarine?" She frowned. "Is this Earth?"

Trillin gazed around. As she watched the walls, they moved. Not the pulsing, living movement of the Endless. The walls briefly stilled, but it wasn't the dead stillness of Earth.

Despite the misty nothing behind the windows, there was no

sign of whatever portal had brought them here, though she vaguely remembered making one, as though the memories belonged to someone else and had only reluctantly been left behind. She pulled them out and turned them over experimentally – yes, she knew how to get out of here again, if either of them needed to.

"No," she said, sending a mouth to whisper in Sian's ear. "We're somewhere different."

"Outside the … windows? Are they windows?" The are-they-windows drifted down the walls towards them and Sian stared. "That … mist … it's like at the university. Our building is in the pocket dimension beneath the non-magical campus. Is this a pocket dimension, too?"

Trillin didn't know. "Not Earth and not the Endless. And you can look at me."

"God, yes." Sian's face split into one of her perfect smiles. Then she frowned. "Are you okay? Back there – you changed."

Trillin looked down at herself and carefully tried to extend feelers from the tips of her fingers. They sprouted as easily as they could in the Endless, or on Earth.

"I'm still changing," she said, and Sian made a frustrated sound.

"You know what I mean! That spell was about to wipe us all out, and then you turned into something different and grabbed it away from me and turned *it* into something different."

Trillin explained what had happened as well as she could, which was not, she felt, very well. But Sian's eyes shone.

"We're somewhere new. Somewhere completely new, where I can look at you as much as I like, and nothing is trying to eat us. Assuming Bunny didn't bring us here as a picnic lunch."

They both looked around. Trillin saw it first: a thickness in one of the walls, with a dozen tiny eyes peering out.

"Sweek!" The eyes disappeared one by one.

"Let's go ahead and assume that means no." Sian smirked at Trillin in a way that made her insides wriggle. Just in case she needed more reminders that she was a changing fragment of the Endless, and not an unchanging human. "Is anyone else coming through?"

"No. The way is closed." How did she know that? Another reluctant memory. Trillin was beginning to suspect it wasn't so much that Bunny didn't want her to know these things, as that it wanted so much not to have to know anything, that it resented the knowledge existing at all. "And the Endless couldn't follow us here, anyway. It's too big, in all of itself. It would have to let fragments escape, and it couldn't guarantee they would want what it wanted."

"Oh, good. We can just lie here, then." Sian was back to smiling.

"Shouldn't we…"

Trillin ran out of words. She'd run out of everything. None of her memories got this far. They'd always stopped as the humans escaped the Endless. She had no knowledge of what happened afterwards.

"What happens now?" she whispered.

"I think that's up to us. Trapped in a pocket dimension created by a fragment on the Endless, suspiciously similar to the magically subterranean university I study at … raises all sorts of questions. Questions we should probably try to answer. Same way I should probably let Havers and poor Jonesy know they didn't explode me just now."

She didn't make any attempts to move.

"That sounds like a good plan," Trillin said. She didn't move, either.

Lying on top of someone meant being *very* close to them. Lying on top of Sian meant…

Trillin gulped.

She could see all the tiny movements Sian's body made. The ones she did on purpose, and the ones her body did by itself. The way her chest rose and fell as she breathed. The flicker of her eyelashes as a stray hair fell across her face. The lines that formed at the edge of her mouth, the warmth of her breath…

"Maybe later," Sian suggested.

Trillin's fingers curled, frond-like. "Sian…"

Something in Sian's expression told Trillin she already knew what she was trying to say, without knowing the words for it. A teasing, tantalising lightness that made her want to find the words as quickly as possible and let it draw out, at the same time.

They were lying so close together. Trillin was still holding herself up, but if she stopped…

Trillin didn't have any memories of how humans acted once they'd saved one another from the Endless. Just that one image of the woman looking back, smirking, *How's that for girlfriend material?*

She could see one way her future rolled out: her and Sian, looking after Bunny as they both learnt more about this strange pocket world. Maybe, slowly, Trillin could find out how humans said the things to each other that she wanted to say too. And practise. And figure out her body, properly, so that when Sian looked at her like … like…

Like she was looking at her now…

Forget memories. Forget what other people did. Forget getting her corporeal form right, and her words. She didn't need words.

Without thinking about it for even a second, Trillin leant down and kissed her.

They touched. Together, but separate. Melding into one another and still staying each their own, edges burning with sensation, two bodies yearning towards one another.

She wasn't perfect. She couldn't help the tentacles that crept out from her form, to sweep that stray hair from Sian's face, and hold her close.

From the way Sian responded, she didn't mind.

Not perfect.

But definitely girlfriend material.

ALSO FROM PAPER ROAD PRESS

THE STONE WĒTĀ
OCTAVIA CADE

When the cold war of data preservation turns bloody – and then explosive – an underground network of scientists, all working in isolation, must decide how much they are willing to risk for the truth. For themselves, their colleagues, and their future. A claustrophobic and compelling cli-fi thriller.

How far would you go to save the world?

NO MAN'S LAND
A.J. FITZWATER

When Dorothea 'Tea' Gray is sent to work on a remote farm, one of many young women left to fill the empty shoes left by fathers and brothers serving in WWII, she finds more than hard work and hot sun in the dusty North Otago nowhere— she finds a magic inside herself she never could have imagined, a way to save her brother in a distant land she never thought she could reach, and a love she never knew existed.

FROM A SHADOW GRAVE
ANDI C. BUCHANAN

Wellington, 1931. Seventeen-year-old Phyllis Symons's body is discovered in the Mount Victoria tunnel construction site.

Eighty years later, Aroha Brooke is determined to save her life.

"Haunting in every sense of the word"
– Charles Payseur, Quick Sip Reviews

Winner of the Sir Julius Vogel Award for Best Novella / Novelette

ALSO FROM PAPER ROAD PRESS

YEAR'S BEST AOTEAROA NEW ZEALAND
SCIENCE FICTION & FANTASY SERIES

This annual anthology series collects together the very best of short speculative fiction
published by writers from Aotearoa New Zealand each year.